THE
LAST
COFFIN

A REDD HERRING NOVEL

THE
LAST
COFFIN

DAVID GEIMAN

WHALER
BOOKS

Buena Vista, VA

1 3 5 7 9 10 8 6 4 2

Library of Congress Control Number: 2022907420

The Last Coffin
David Geiman

p. cm.
1. Fiction: Mystery & Detective—General
2. Fiction: Mystery & Detective—Police Procedural
3. Fiction: Thrillers—Crime

I. Geiman, David, 1944– II. Title.
ISBN 13: 978-1-7378864-8-8 (hardcover : alk. paper)
ISBN 13: 978-1-7378864-6-4 (softcover : alk. paper)
ISBN 13: 978-1-7378864-7-1 (ebook)

Design and Layout by Karen Bowen

Whaler Books
An imprint of
Mariner Media, Inc.
131 West 21st Street
Buena Vista, VA 24416
Tel: 540-264-0021
www.marinermedia.com

Printed in the United States of America

This book is printed on acid-free paper meeting the requirements of the American Standard for Permanence of Paper for Printed Library Materials.

Contents

Part One

David Geiman

From: Messenger25092018gmt10@nordVPN
Date: September 22, 2018
To: WBA55@CennFarm.com
Subject: Finances and Remuneration

Sir:

This letter is in response to your recent restructuring
and financing initiatives. We must insist that any
efforts to draw down your equity or cash positions
are unacceptable in light of your upcoming
obligations as to remuneration for the deaths
in northern Iraq on July 30, 2016. We are in the
process of setting up mechanisms for payment and
we look forward to your immediate and appropriate
response.

Remunerations Committee
Alliance for International Human Rights

From: Messenger07102018@nordVPN
Date: October 6, 2018, 04:30
To: WBA55@CennFarm.com
Subject: Finances and Remuneration

Sir:

We have not received a response to our email to you
of September 22, 2018. A copy is attached.

In addition, we have received notice that your refinancing efforts are continuing in contravention of our request to put those efforts on hold, given the adverse effect such restructuring would have on our client's interests.

Attached you will find one photograph of the death scene in northern Iraq, which is part of the evidence in our case.

Attached you will also find a photograph of a reconstructed model of the same scene which will be utilized for publicity purposes later today.

Given the milieu in which we must pursue these remunerations, we hope that the second scene will remind you of the potentially unfortunate reputational consequences that could attach to you and your businesses should you continue to attempt to move and otherwise utilize assets.

Remunerations Committee
Alliance for International Human Rights

Att: pdf.092218
Photo 1.sxl
Photo 2.sxl

1

The First Coffin

The first coffin was found on the railroad tracks Saturday, October 6th. It was sitting crosswise with the head of the coffin pointing east toward Washington, DC, Europe, the Middle East.

The fact that it was found that morning was an anomaly. The tracks belonged to a short line railroad that connected the larger main railroad in the town of Staunton, Virginia, to three or four communities to the north. The trains normally didn't run on Saturday. Charlie Green, the retired Norfolk & Western engineer who came upon the coffin, was now the engineer for this short line, on the limited days it runs.

He considered moving the coffin from the tracks, but there are rules about things found on railroad tracks and he opted to follow them this morning. Might the coffin actually contain a body? It was securely fastened shut with rows of screws making examination of the contents impossible without tools.

He called the Augusta County sheriff's department. The dispatcher who answered passed Charlie's call on to Sheriff Herring who took down the details of the location. Herring's office was less than ten minutes from where Green waited on the tracks.

Deputy Roddie Roudabush, who had just returned from a domestic dispute call, rode shotgun with Sheriff Herring. The coffin was on the tracks in a shallow cut just north of the town of Verona. An unpaved road led to a railroad crossing a hundred yards or more from the coffin, but the crossing was now blocked by the stalled train.

Herring parked his official Ford SUV, and he and Roudabush walked in the scruffy grass alongside the train to the coffin blocking its path. The sluggish old Norfolk & Western engine had seen better days. It wheezed on and off as if one or more of the cylinders couldn't quite catch its breath. It pulled ten covered hopper cars filled with corn from central Ohio, bound for a poultry feed mill in the town of Harrisonburg, twenty-five miles north. By the time the two officers arrived, several other people had gathered at the site. They'd also been unable to cross the tracks and were curious about the blockage.

"So, what do we have here?" asked Herring, of no one in particular.

"Who the hell knows?" replied Charlie. "An early Halloween prank? I would liked to have just pushed it out of the way with the engine, but I don't know what's in it. It's heavy as hell. And the bosses would have a fit if I didn't follow the rules and regulations."

Herring studied it. "There might be a body in it."

"There is that, I guess," agreed Charlie.

Roudabush tried to budge one end of the coffin, then tried to pick it up. "Jeez, what does it have in it, bricks? And how in the hell did it get here?"

"Well let's get it open," said Herring. "Roddie, run back and get the toolbox out of my car. Screwdriver and pry bar, at least."

A few minutes later, with the use of a Phillips, the screws were out and the lid of the coffin was loose.

"What the hell? I've heard of a box of rocks but not a box of sand!" exclaimed Charlie when he saw the contents.

Herring began to scrape the sand around with gloved hands to see what else was in there. Down an inch or so he unearthed some heavy black plastic material that resembled the stuff body bags are made of. He could feel a rounded surface underneath near the top and began clearing the sand away more deliberately.

Indeed it was a body bag! With three sturdy woven lifting handles on each side. Once the sand had been scooped out enough to get a hold of the handles, the sheriff asked the bystanders to help move the bag out onto the grassy patch beside the track. They hadn't been able to take their eyes off of it and were now surprised how easy it was to lift. Everyone's heard about dead weight, and they expected it to be heavy. Herring shook the top end of the bag to get the sand out of the zipper and slowly opened it from the top about halfway down. The mummy-like object inside was shrouded in white cotton fabric. Herring hesitantly lifted and unwound the strips of cloth, exposing the upper torso of an adult male mannequin.

A layer of paper was taped over the mannequin's eyes. Under the paper was a layer of cardboard and a thin sheet of bubble wrap. Beneath the layers, the eyes were covered by a photograph of two wide-open eyes that looked terrified. Herring took several photographs of the face with his phone and then put the protective coverings back in place and taped them back down. He zipped the bag open further.

At the waist was another piece of tape securing more layers of cardboard and packing material. The smooth crotch of the mannequin was covered with a piece of clear plastic tape that held a picture of male genitals in place. No one said a word.

Herring zipped the bag closed. He had no clue what such an assembly might mean. It exceeded the normal high school and college pranks he'd seen many times. This level of obscenity went beyond the typical pornographic. Someone was sending someone a message with the coffin, the bag, the jarring personification.

"Let's get the coffin off of the tracks so Charlie here can get on his way. A couple of you help us carry the bag and put it in the back of my vehicle. I guess it's useless to ask you not to talk about this, but I'd appreciate you keeping quiet while we do a little checking."

He wasn't sure why he bothered to make that request. They'd be on their cell phones before they left the crossing, and several had probably taken photos while he was opening the bag and concentrating on the chore at hand. Most likely they had already shared some account of it on Facebook or Instagram.

Several men took hold of the coffin and tipped it to let the weight of the sand spill out beside the tracks. As the box emptied, a small burlap sack a little bigger than a cornhole beanbag surfaced. It was tied shut with a short piece of plastic twine. Herring picked it up and tossed it up and down in his palm a few times.

He took an evidence bag from his back pocket and collected a sample of the sand. A few of the men helped carry the coffin back to the SUV. Herring realized at this point, close to eleven in the morning, that he should have previously cordoned off the area and called a technician to check for fingerprints, but it was too late now.

When they got back to the department, Herring had Roddie help carry the coffin to an evidence prep room down the hall from his office. They removed the body bag with the mannequin and placed it on a table.

"We'll need to photograph this thing, and check to see if there is a manufacturer's name or something else on the mannequin that tells us where it might have come from. Where do you buy something like this? And check the body bag too. What kind it is, where it was made?"

"Can this wait until Monday, Redd?" asked Roddie. "I'm supposed to be off this afternoon for apple picking with Barb and the kids. I'll get my ass chewed if I miss it. She has it in her head to make old-fashioned apple butter and has rounded up her cousins from over by Monterey. She found an old iron kettle at the antique mall in Verona, and a bunch of apple peelers and the whole damn mess."

"Hmm…" mused the sheriff. He had forgotten about Roddie wanting the afternoon off.

"Do you know how apple butter used to be made?" Without waiting for an answer Roddie continued, "You pick all the apples first, then you make cider out of a bunch. I guess we will just buy that. And then you peel God-only-knows how many apples and core them out, and then you heat up the cider in the ancient kettle over a wood fire, which reminds me I need to split some more oak. There goes half the wood for the winter. And then you boil the damn cider and keep putting in apples, and then you stir the damn mix for like twelve hours and keep it boiling along. And I guess you put in sugar and spices or whatever. Her aunt has a recipe. And you keep stirring it with this long wooden thing she found somewhere so you don't have to be too close to the fire, and then you have to cool it and can it and by then I bet every jar of apple butter has cost twenty dollars. And…"

"Roddie! It's fine to take the afternoon off. Go ahead. It's not like we have a murder here. See you Monday." Redd had in mind that Roddie might just as soon be asked to stay, so he could get out of the apple butter obligation.

Roddie grimaced, mock-saluted the sheriff and headed out the door. He lived off of old Highway 250 just before Church-ville in a two-story frame house on two acres of land. His wife, Barb, a slightly stout energetic woman two years Roddie's senior, was constantly looking for ways to honor the good-old-days in their home. Braiding her own rugs, planting a vegetable garden, filling the pantry with foods she had canned for the winter. She was one of the few serious gardeners left in the county, other than the Mennonites and Amish. She made her own pickles, baked pies, and was regarded in the community as a very good cook. Roddie didn't seem to appreciate how good he had it. In a county that topped state statistics for obesity, Roddie was still fit and muscular and carried only 170 pounds on his six-foot frame. At forty, he had a full head of dark hair with only a few grey strands and looked younger than his age. Everyone reck-oned that the constant rotation of chores on Barb's honey-do list contributed to his fitness. Roddie reckoned that the chores just kept him from watching sports, even on Sunday afternoons in the winter.

After Roddie took off, the sheriff unzipped the bag again and examined the mannequin more closely. This near-perfect male replica was slim with nicely proportioned shoulders, a flat stomach and a slightly rounded butt. It reminded him of the mannequins in the department stores of his youth, when everyone was thirty or forty pounds lighter. He couldn't imagine clothes that fit this mannequin fitting anyone he knew now, not even Roddie.

Rolling it over revealed a hole low on the buttocks for mounting it on a display stand. There were some Chinese language characters stamped near the hole, as well as the English word *Jinta* next to *J-103 M*, apparently a design number. Research as to the origin and availability could be done online once he returned to his office.

He snapped a few more photos, including some of the numbers and name, rewrapped the mannequin, and zipped it back into the bag. The bag itself had a small label saying *DeXi* and an illegible number. More to research.

He took a zip tie from a shelf and pulled it through the zipper tab and then through a metal hook just above the end of the zipper to lock the bag shut. He wrote REDD and DO NOT OPEN on a label and secured it to the zip tie. Regrettably, so many had already seen the taped-on genitalia when it was uncovered at the tracks. He didn't want to hear the inevitable cracks and speculation that would come from a bunch of guys in the office. There are only male deputies in his patrol division, but women work in the civil and court divisions, and they don't need to see it either.

The coffin was on the floor. Herring put the cover back on, taped it shut with blue tape, labeled it. The room has shelves on two walls and a large amount of storage space for everything from stolen hunting trophies to outboard engines. And there is a secure parking lot next to the building that safeguards stolen cars, boats, four-wheelers, and other items. He placed the body bag on a shelf in the evidence prep room and locked the door on his way out.

Herring pulled up Google as soon as he got back to his desk. He typed in mannequins. His very first search revealed that the mannequin was indeed from China and could be bought for eighty-nine dollars each in lots of five hundred. Further searches revealed much more than he needed to know. *Mannequin Madness* discussed the collection of mannequins as a hobby, and the names of well-regarded manufacturers mostly from days-gone-by whose mannequins sold for a thousand dollars, not eighty-nine. He also learned that the hole in the butt was called a butt tube. And that you could buy mannequins with high-quality insertable eyes of different colors from dozens of sources. Body bags were readily available from numerous websites. It occurred to him that the sheriff's department had never ordered any. They'd always been supplied by the coroner's office. They were cheap. The model he had just tagged was only thirty-four dollars plus shipping.

He was interrupted by a call from Annie Laurie, the department's receptionist, dispatcher, mother figure, and weekend cookie provider. "Redd, I have Mr. Wilson for you." *Lord, help me,* thought Redd. *So soon.* Charles Austin Wilson, the Chairman of the Board of Supervisors.

"Herring, what in heaven's name are you up to? My phone is ringing off the hook."

Amused by the dated figure of speech, and playing the innocent, Herring responded, "What are you talking about?"

"You know what I'm talking about. You and that pornographic doll. It's all over the internet."

"Okay, settle down. That should not have gotten out there. We had an incident—"

Before he could finish, he was interrupted by Wilson.

"An incident?! It looks like state-sponsored pornography to me. You, you need to get that removed right now!"

Wilson was a member of one of the older families in the county, and although he claimed to be a descendant of Woodrow Wilson, he was not. Unless you take into account the kindred spirit of racism. A reporter from a local weekly paper once referred to him as a "stillborn" Christian as opposed to a "born again" Christian because of his narrow views on morality and the role of the church in society. He was not in total denial of evolution, but he did put a restricted timeline on it. And while not a flat-earth proponent, he was still suspicious of the curvature.

Officially, Herring did not report to the supervisors. Like most sheriffs across the country, he had been elected directly by the citizens of the county. But as the citizens' elected representatives, the board was a de facto set of superiors who could make his life miserable. They already had from time to time.

"Charles Austin," responded Herring, "this is most likely a disgusting prank by some high school or college kids, and we had no reason to believe anything like this would be in the coffin on the track."

"Well, you need to clear it up."

"We are on top of it."

Herring filled him in the best he could between interruptions and blustering comments about responsibility and repercussions. Finally he claimed he had an emergency call coming in and hung up. Wilson's call would not be the only call. To escape the scourge, he would have to leave the office. Poor Annie Laurie would be left to field the calls and send them on to his voice mail or take messages.

Herring was not officially on duty for the weekend. He had come in to follow up on the endless paperwork from the previous week. And he wanted to review new materials generated by the courts on the handling of gender-neutral prisoners. Unlike several of the older deputies, he had no problem with the gender issues. He was lucky to have been raised by a uniquely liberal and forgiving mother whose trait of tolerance had become an intrinsic part of his character.

Reddford Herring was just shy of sixty and had been sheriff of the county for nearly fifteen years. He had grown up on one of the last true family farms in Augusta County, a farm that had been lost to the bank in the financial and agricultural crisis of the early 1980s. Herring wasn't interested in farming as a career. He had been in college in a prelaw program at the time of the loss. It did not register as deeply with him as it probably should have. His father had worked the farm part-time and worked in town by necessity as well. Herring had not grasped the sense of failure and loss that descended on his father, and the depression that took years to overcome.

By the time Herring finished college in 1982 he was no longer sure he wanted to pursue a legal career. Jobs were hard to come by, so he enlisted in the army. It suited him, and he stayed in until 1990. He had been a part of Reagan's military buildup to smother the Soviet Union. That smothering could have been accomplished with a pillow, rather than the blanket of weapons and men that Congress funded during the decade. But part of that effort was an army process called *Lessons Learned.* All actions were analyzed and debriefed upon completion, and the lessons learned applied to the next set of operations. Herring loved the analysis and the applications. He excelled.

A love of reading was inherited from his grandfather. Herring read everything from classic novels to thrillers to history. Partly because of his military training he had a special interest in World War I. He studied the causes and the mind-lessness of the Western front with the trench warfare that took so many lives without accomplishing anything. He occasionally gave guest lectures at both the high school and college level, but he found the students' interest in history to be declining in the last twenty years.

In 1990, at five feet eleven and 180 pounds, Herring had a thirty-three-inch waist, broad shoulders, and an erect carriage. He was a disciplined career-military-type man whose edges had been softened. He had never thought of himself as especially handsome, but women thought he undersold himself. He had a solid jaw, a nose just slightly reminiscent of some supposed Italian heritage, brown eyes that tended to grey in some light. His hair was dark brown and quite thick, so he thought he would never be bald. But he had not looked closely enough at the photographs of his maternal grandfather.

He had an innate sense of curiosity, learned a lot from listening, and came across as a keeper of secrets. He met Mary Lyon when she transferred to the new combined high school in her senior year. They fell in love in a few short weeks, dated through college. He went to the University of Virginia on a scholarship, and Mary transferred there from Mary Washington, the sister school, when that became an option. She was also on a scholarship and studied to be a schoolteacher. They got married when they graduated.

Two years into their marriage, there was no child on the way. A set of tests revealed that Mary would never be able to conceive because she had been born with an abnormally-shaped uterus. There was no way to alter the shape or effect a pregnancy. They discussed adoption but kept postponing a decision. In time the decision was made by default.

Their marriage was happy and as balanced as could be hoped for, when one evening Mary collapsed in the kitchen. Within six weeks, she was dead from a rare form of lung cancer. She had never smoked. For the first time in thirty-five years, except for time spent in military training, Herring now lived alone. He missed Mary and their lively conversations. They had traveled to Europe on occasion, mainly as part of classroom trips. Mary engendered in him a sense of worldliness that the military had not, in spite of his role in the more managerial aspects of preparing for war and sometimes peace.

Herring still weighed 180 pounds, but now his waist was thirty-five inches, his shoulders were slightly less broad, and his doctor told him his Body Mass Index was borderline. He would do well to lose ten pounds.

David Geiman

From: Messenger21102018@nordVPN
Date: October 20, 2018, 04:30
To: WBA55@CennFarm.com
Subject: Finances and Remuneration

Sir:

We must once again express our regrets that we
have had no response to our earlier communications
to you, and we are aware that you are continuing
with financial restructuring, the proposed outcome
of which would be detrimental to our client's
interests.

We are aware that you may not have been available
to view the earlier scene which we provided. In that
case, we are providing another reminder today,
and photographs of the original death and the first
reminder are both attached below.

We must insist on a cessation of restructuring and a
response to that effect immediately.

Remuneration Committee
Alliance for International Human Rights

Att: Photo 1.sxl
Photo 2.sxl

2

The Second Coffin

On a cooler sunny Saturday near the end of October, a call came into the sheriff's office around ten in the morning. Two teenagers on four-wheelers had been illegally trying to ride on the train rails. They had come across another coffin on the tracks not far from the spot of the first, near Verona. They didn't mention they had been riding on the rails, didn't give their names, didn't give phone numbers. Naïve to the fact that caller ID had already identified them, they left the tracks and rode back home.

This time Sheriff Herring went out alone, took along a shovel and his tool bag and parked at the crossing as he had done before. He asked Annie Laurie to let Roddie know where he was headed.

A smooth pine coffin like the first was placed in roughly the same position on the tracks. This one was also too heavy to move. Herring had thought to put a power drill with a Phillips screwdriver attachment in his tool bag this go round. The box was open in no time.

This one contained brownish round pea gravel instead of sand. He brushed aside some gravel and quickly found the zipper of another body bag that appeared to hold another mannequin. He scooped out enough of the gravel to get at the handles and gently lifted the bag and laid it beside the tracks.

The mannequin was male, about the size of an adolescent this time. The body was shrouded in white cotton material, wound around in layers. The face was once again taped over. Beneath layers of plastic there was a picture of a pair of terror-filled eyes. Herring pulled out his phone and scrolled to the photos of the first mannequin and verified that the eyes had the same expression.

Further down in the crotch area there was just the smooth surface of a normal mannequin, no tape this time, no photograph. This mannequin was in much worse condition than the one from two weeks earlier. It appeared to have been stored somewhere dusty or dirty and there were cracks in the surface of the body as if it had rolled around in transport.

Herring managed to shovel most of the gravel out of the coffin, enabling him to slide it off the tracks so that a train could pass if one came along. He pried a loose board off the coffin and put some of the gravel into a Ziplock. It took two trips to get the board, the gravel, and the body bag with its contents back to the SUV. He'd send a couple deputies back to pick up the box.

He had not thought much about the first coffin over the past two weeks. The flurry of emails and calls about the photos of the male genitalia had slowed. A flash flood in town from a night of heavy rain had sidetracked everyone's attention.

Initially Herring had looked on the first coffin incident as foreboding. But when nothing further developed, he'd chalked it up to a prank, albeit a sophisticated one. Maybe college students could pull it off?

But with the arrival of the second coffin, he was back to his initial thinking. It would have taken at least four people to move the heavy box when it was full, a shop in which to assemble it, or at least some tools. There was lumber to purchase, sand, mannequin, and a truck to haul it all to the site. If that's how it had been done, and that many people had been involved, it seemed unlikely that all of them could have kept it a secret. And wasn't the point of a prank to celebrate it with your friends?

A second coffin, almost identical to the first, in the same location, with a distinctly different mannequin, eyes also showing terror. It made no sense to Herring. And why sand in the first coffin and pea gravel in this one? It all pointed to a lot of work, a lot of organization, and a team effort. The more he thought about it, the more macabre it felt. Maybe that was the intent. Halloween was just a week or so away. Horror movies abound, talk of zombies so common you'd think they were real.

Blaine Wortham was just pulling into the parking lot when Herring got back to the department. Blaine was another of his deputies, fondly known as Blaine the Man. He was a sharp dresser, eschewing the local Carhartt and denims for the preppier khakis and button-down. He kept a word-of-the-day calendar on his desk and made a point of dropping the word into conversation throughout the day, appropriate or not.

Herring had Wortham help him carry the second bag into the same storage area as the first. He pulled the mannequin out to photograph it from all angles. The butt tube was looser and showed signs of having been caulked or glued back into place. The surface was rougher, and he could not make out the name or model numbers. An odd sense of empathy came across Herring. This mannequin embodied weariness and abuse.

He bagged it up, zip-tied the zipper, put his name and a note on the mannequin and the bag, and put it on the shelf with the first one. He pondered them for a few minutes before walking down the hall to Annie Laurie's desk.

"Annie, do we still have any of those game cameras that we used to use for out-of-season hunting and baiting?"

She thought so. It took her about a half hour but she brought him a box holding a Wildgame Innovations camera including straps and directions. She even brought along a box of batteries, eight of which were needed.

Herring mounted the camera near the tracks, close to where the coffins had been found.

He had always been a fan of puzzles. He had begun to rule out prank. A week after the second coffin appeared he made a list of things to look into relative to the mysteries. For a while he had wondered if some fraternity at the University of Virginia might have put it together as a way to mess with the rubes in the valley, but that seemed fairly unlikely given the complexity.

The temperature had turned cooler, and Herring spent his evenings at home in front of a cozy fire. He surfed the internet for examples of mannequins used as substitutes for humans or as ritualistic symbols. One of the more interesting entries came from a tome on early Chinese religions. It discussed the Daoist use of mannequins as human substitutes to absorb the sufferings of the recently dead to keep them from returning to haunt the living.

Out of curiosity, he googled "use of sand and stones in rituals." He learned that sand was used in all types of ceremonies including the mixing of sands as a ritual in some marriage rites. There were sand painting ceremonies where the "dry sand" paintings were requests to the gods for help and healing. He had almost forgotten about the burlap bag of sand in the first coffin. He typed in "bags of sand." Sandbags to hold back flood waters came up, some military uses, and a reference to small bags of sand as torture devices used by ISIS in northeastern Syria and Iraq. They were tied to the victim's penis causing enormous pain and damage.

He wondered if the absence of a picture of genitalia on the second mannequin related to that. Might the battered mannequin in the second coffin have represented a victim of such torture? Could the combination of a male figure with genitalia and one without, along with the sandbag and the practice of shrouding, point to a Middle Eastern connection?

He also looked into the equally diverse use of stones. From large stone installations such as Stonehenge, to places on the Irish and Welsh coasts that sported healing stones, to long discussions of crystals and their healing powers. By the end of the second night of research Herring had had enough of sand and stone. He didn't feel that he had learned anything of use.

It was a day before Halloween and the camera was in place. If another coffin or mannequin showed up on the tracks there would be pictures. He had gone back to Annie Laurie and gotten a second game camera to hide where it would photograph anyone who used the railroad crossing. And coffins or not, it was trick-or-treat time. He would be busy with stupid human ruses, illegal fireworks, and whatever shenanigans the locals could dream up.

The burning oak tree in the park was the most surprising Halloween site. A prankster lit the toilet paper he had draped around the tree. Instead of creating the sparkling necklace of toilet paper that he had envisioned, the dry leaves caught fire and turned the tree into a giant torch.

There were no coffins on the track, no unusual images on the game cameras. Normal comings and goings of an occasional short train with some hopper cars of grain or loads of pine framing lumber from Canada or the far west. A few deer, some skunks, two foxes, a fat groundhog. A small black bear sat on one of the rails for a few minutes before waddling on.

Herring thought perhaps the whole escapade was over.

David Geiman

From: Messenger05112018@nordVPN
Date: November 3, 2018, 04:30
To: WBA55@CennFarm.com
Subject: Finances and Remuneration—Final

Sir:

We have received your short response that stated
your belief that all of the actions to date constitute
a hoax and a lack of ability or determination to
follow through. We wish to assure you that nothing
could be further from the truth. While we wish no
harm to you physically, we are willing to use such
methods as seem appropriate to assure the financial
remuneration due your victims' families.

Our primary focus at the moment is to prevent the
transfer of funds out of your estate. We have thus
far not identified you to the general public. We are
going to provide for you, the third exhibition of our
knowledge of your actions in a more public setting
later this morning. If we do not have assurances that
the restructuring of your finances has ceased within
a week, we will make all of the photographs public
along with supporting details.

Remuneration Committee
Alliance for International Human Rights

Att: Photo 1.sxl
        Photo 2.sxl

3

The Third Coffin

The first Saturday in November, Herring was awakened at four in the morning by a call from the night dispatcher. "I thought I should call you. We had a call a few minutes ago from Byron Roster—the guy who opened that new bakery?"

"Yes, I know who you mean."

"Well, because of the flood a couple of weeks ago, some of the streets are still closed and he has to come in by the train station, you know, up on the hill, with the crooked platform?"

Of course, Herring knew. There was only one train station, and it had always been up on the hill and had always had a famous curved platform designed by Stanford White. And now one train a day stopped, never on time, from Chicago in one direction and Washington and New York in the other. Did anyone have a map and know that Staunton and Washington were not on the direct route from Chicago to New York?

"Yes, I know, what does Byron need?"

"Well, he always comes in early to start baking, and he says there appears to be a coffin on the road near the terminal building, sort of where people park. I thought I should call you."

"Okay, is anybody in right now?"

"No, Roddie was here but a call came in about a car hitting a deer out on 340."

"Okay, I'll head in myself now. Call Roddie and tell him if the deer thing is not serious to head back to the train station right away."

"Yes sir, will do."

Herring realized that in his groggy state he had not asked the night dispatcher's name. He could also have asked the dispatcher to call someone on the state police force to come over and cover for him. But that hadn't occurred to him either.

He pulled on civilian clothes and jumped in the Ford and headed to town. It would take about fifteen minutes, first north on 42 and then a quick ten minutes through Churchville into Staunton from the west. He thought about using lights and siren but couldn't justify it. This was most likely just another wooden coffin with another strange mannequin in it.

When he got to the train station, Roddie had not arrived, and there wasn't a soul around. It was four thirty in the morning, and it was still as dark as midnight. The sun wouldn't come up until seven. He could see the coffin on the ground up near the terminal. It was in a cobblestone parking area, the only cobblestone parking lot Herring knew of anywhere in Virginia. It's where you waited if you were waiting on the train. He was not sure why Byron would have seen it, but there was a yellow sodium light over that portion of the lot, and he supposed if you glanced in that direction, you'd spot it. Byron was probably aware of the earlier coffin incidents, making it more likely that this one would catch his eye.

He pulled up close and directed his low beams on the box. He took his tools out of the back. The coffin was similar to the first two, slightly wider and a bit deeper as if made for an obese individual. He had no trouble removing the lid. This coffin was only partially filled with sand and the body bag appeared to be larger than the earlier two. He scooped out enough sand to get to the handles and removed the bag.

There were two mannequins. One was an adult size female shrouded in white fabric. Bound around her chest was a swaddled mannequin of a baby. The eyes of the woman were taped over in what was becoming the usual fashion. When Herring removed the covering to expose the expected photograph, eyes of infinite sadness stared back at him. Herring zipped the bag closed and stood up.

4

Autumn Break

Herring could not decide what, if anything, he should do. It was hard to ignore the unmistakable message that somebody, somewhere was intent on warning someone about something. But no one had called him. There had been a brief flurry of internet activity after the first coffin was found, but that had died down after the floods. The second discovery had produced a few days of Facebook sharing and a few calls from parents, but that's all.

Maybe he should have paid more attention to the shrouding. He knew about Muslim burial practices from his time in the army. The bodies are washed and wrapped and quickly interred in coffins with no bottoms, so the bodies can decompose in the earth naturally. But as far as he knew, there were no Muslims in the county, and these boxes had bottoms.

He built a matrix to help organize his thoughts. In the first column he put location:

Train tracks
Train tracks
Train station

In the second he noted the time and who found the boxes:

10 a.m. Discovered by train engineer. Time of placement, unknown.
Mid-morning. Kids on four wheelers. Time of placement, unknown.
4 a.m. Baker. Time of placement, unknown, but probably narrower window.

Third he noted the filler material:

Sand
Smooth pea gravel
Sand

Then he moved on to the mannequins themselves:

Ordinary male, good condition with frightened eyes.
Younger male, weathered or abused, with frightened
eyes.
Adult female, baby on chest, sad eyes on adult.

He then remembered the coffin differences:

Normal. Pine.
Normal. Pine.
Larger, deeper. Pine.

He went on to the circumstances. The first coffin was found
by an engineer on a morning when the train would not have
normally run. But eventually one would have come through.
The second coffin was found by a couple of kids on four wheelers. The third coffin appeared in a much more public place,

still related to trains, as if there was an urgency to its discovery. Someone would certainly see it at dawn. As it turned out, it had been discovered even earlier.

Could the details of these seemingly random discoveries be happenstance, secondary to the intentions of the person placing the coffins? If this person truly wanted to send a message, would they rely on serendipity? Herring felt their messages would have been more targeted. These coffin displays were telling us something else. A threat? A warning of public exposure?

Beyond the blatant symbolism of coffins and body bags, and the use of plain pine boxes like coffins of yore, the only other possible symbols were in the sand and stone. Perhaps he had overlooked something in his research.

It was only a week until Thanksgiving. Roddie had invited Herring to have a turkey dinner with his family. Barb had already made real cranberry sauce and a spice mixture for mulling cider. She had plans for four kinds of pies, and her homemade crusts were waiting in the freezer.

The Killer

The killer did not set out on Friday morning with the intent of killing. But requests and pressure had not been working, and action was needed now. Commitments had to be honored. The killer had an older model Smith & Wesson .22-caliber that was not registered and didn't have a serial number, but it still worked. These types of guns are the preferred ones for contract killers due to portability, low noise level, and lack of blood spatter so the killer doesn't get covered with blood or brain matter. The killer hoped that with Ashby's military background he would be impressed by the show of strength.

5

More Coffins

It was Saturday afternoon. Herring was at home stacking firewood when a call came from Annie Laurie.

"Redd, I thought I'd better call you. I just had a call from a Kathryn Ashby. I think you know of her—the daughter of Colonel Winston Ashby? He has the big Angus farm west of town."

"Yes." Herring knew of the Ashby family, had seen them around, but didn't really know them.

"Well, she just got back to the farm I guess, and she said Winston's plane is parked there by the hangar, but he and his wife Caroline are not around anywhere. I didn't understand the entire sequence, but she said Winston and Caroline were supposed to have left from the Shenandoah Valley Airport to fly to Dulles for a flight to Europe Friday afternoon."

"Really? She just got back to the farm? Where has she been?"

"She said she had gone camping in West Virginia on Thursday and only came back today because she had an upset stomach. She wasn't due back until tomorrow."

"What did you tell her?"

"I told her I would call you and have someone get back to her."

"Did she seem upset?"

"Not overly, but she couldn't understand why the plane would be there when she knew they were headed to Europe. She said she looked around, and the plane was chocked with those things by the tires, but not tied down. She looked inside and their luggage was there in the back."

"Did she go up to the house?"

"She said she was calling from the house."

"Okay, Annie, can you call her back and tell her I'll be out shortly? Find out where she'll be so I can meet her. Does she live on the farm?"

"I didn't ask, but I guess she must. It didn't sound like she lives in her dad's house though."

"Are you leaving work soon?"

"In a minute. But I can wait if you need me to."

"No. Just text me a number where I can reach Miss Ashby and you can take off. Thanks."

Herring changed out of his work jeans and into his uniform and headed to the Ashby farm. He expected nothing much more than a misunderstanding. Airplanes break down frequently and just because the Ashbys hadn't taken off yet didn't mean they were in trouble. Maybe Winston had driven somewhere to get a mechanic. Herring had no idea what level of mechanic qualified as an airplane mechanic, or where you might find one. Presumably at airports.

It took him about twenty minutes to get out to the farm. A rolling pastoral scene, common to the valley, stretched across the green landscape of wooden fences, outbuildings, and cattle. An impressive farm entrance led up a long gravel lane, and Herring could see the plane parked in front of a barn. A paved runway extended from the state highway to a spot well beyond the plane.

He was to meet Kathryn Ashby at the barn. He had seen her around town but had never spoken with her. She taught part-time at the University of Virginia across the mountain in Charlottesville, and as far as he knew she didn't socialize much with locals.

He pulled up to the barn where a black Celebration Farms pickup was parked. Kathryn Ashby was in the cab. He had found Kathryn very attractive when he glimpsed her in town. But at the moment he couldn't tell much about her. She had a hoodie pulled fairly tightly around her head and was wearing sunglasses. Her face was mostly concealed. But he could see that she looked pale, washed out. She did not get out. Herring introduced himself.

"Sheriff, I apologize, but I got sick from some bad mushrooms. My stomach is giving me a fit. I don't know where my father and Caroline could be. They should have been in Europe by now. I looked around in this barn and up at the house but haven't felt well enough to look all over the farm. I have to go back to my house and lie down. Can I get you to check around the farm? Here are keys to all of the gates and barns. They are numbered."

She started her truck. "I'm really sorry. Call me. Here's my cell number." She handed him a piece of paper and pulled away.

This was a strange encounter for such a serious-sounding matter. But under the circumstances of Kathryn's illness Herring guessed it made sense. He decided to start at the barns nearest the plane. The first was actually a hangar for the King Air that was parked just outside its doors. The plane's wheels were chocked as Kathryn had said. The wooden blocks had a rope threaded through them to make the chocks easy to carry. Planes at airports worldwide are chocked in the same manner. He would look in the plane later since Kathryn had already told Annie Laurie that the plane was empty except for luggage.

The hangar was clean. The interior was painted white. Fire extinguishers were hanging on the walls in several places. The spotless floor was some type of highly polished concrete. Not a speck of dust anywhere. There were two closet-like cabinets standing by the back wall, both locked. A door opened into an office on one side. No one was in there.

To the left of the hangar was a large equipment shed with tractors, haying equipment, cattle trailers, pickup trucks. Herring located a light switch so he could see inside the tractor cabs and cattle trailers. No bodies, no evidence.

He walked over to a smaller shed. He found the key and opened the door to what looked like a veterinary and processing shop. It connected to a set of indoor pens where a couple animals were lying around in straw bedding, apparently recovering from ailments. There were no good hiding places in this complex, for people or bodies.

He wished he had asked Kathryn for a map or a diagram of the farm. In spite of the vast acreage, it was easy to trace its boundaries. The well-maintained fencing was distinctive, and the buildings were all painted the same shade of grey-black. There were sorting pens and what looked like a small show barn further up the road he'd come in on. He decided to investigate that next.

This facility looked as if it might measure seventy-five by seventy-five. It was about the same height as the other buildings, enclosed on all sides. There were gravel parking spaces in front and to one side, and what appeared to be a small office area in the front. There was a lettered sign on the door that read "Arena."

The door led to a short hallway with an open office area to the left, and doors to restrooms on the right. The office held a desk and a number of comfortable chairs. *Nice*, thought Herring. Maybe this was a business meeting area for when the farm held on-site sales of its animals. Must not have been used recently as there was a layer of dust on all of the furniture.

At the back of the office area, double doors gave way to an open space. Herring found a switch for banks of ceiling lights that illuminated a small arena. The seating was ranked like a basketball stadium but with a sawdust floor. To the back, the rows of seating were divided to allow for an entryway such as football players might burst through to enter the playing field.

In the middle of this small stadium were two pine coffins.

Both were screwed shut in the same manner as the other three had been. He sensed that these two contained the bodies of Ashby and his wife Caroline, which established this as a probable crime scene. So he decided to follow conventions and do only a cursory determination before calling in technical help. He returned to his SUV and found disposable gloves and took a screwdriver and zip ties from his toolbox. It occurred to him that he had already opened doors all over the farm with no gloves on. He had left fingerprints and tire tracks on most of the access points. Given the gravel, it probably didn't matter about the tires, but the door handles might matter.

He went back into the arena, noticing now that the sawdust had previously been raked around the coffins so that no footprints were visible. He stepped lightly to the side of the coffin on the right and loosened the screws. He slid the lid over onto the top of the other coffin and looked inside. A familiar body bag, but no sand or stone. He threaded a zip tie through the hole in the zipper pull so as not to disturb any fingerprints that might be there. He pulled the zipper down slightly. The body was wrapped completely in soft cotton sheeting leaving only the eyes visible. Herring moved the material just enough to determine that this was undeniably Caroline Ashby.

He zipped her up and slid the lid back in place, deciding not to open the second coffin. He tested it for weight. It was quite heavy.

The county did not maintain its own forensics team because the demand for this type of examination was rare. The state police department managed cases of this sort for them. He called from his car and explained what he had found. Herring arranged for a crime scene specialist to come out to inspect the area and take the bodies for examination and autopsies.

6

Wendell Berry

Due to the fact that the earlier, pretty much identical coffins had been found on the railroad tracks, Herring decided to also call the FBI. These bodies were a local matter, but crimes associated with railroads, even loosely, had special standing due to interstate commerce and federal regulations.

The field agent who answered put Herring on hold when he heard what he was calling about. In spite of what is often written, Herring had not found it difficult to work with the FBI over the years. They had resources that he could only dream of and had assisted him on several cases in the past where jurisdiction was uncertain. Being so close to West Virginia, criminals could easily fall into a federal category by going back and forth between the states. He only knew a little about Colonel Ashby, but he didn't think of him as particularly interesting to the FBI.

Soon Wendell Berry was on the line, Herring's long-time friend and principal contact at the FBI. He was short and to the point. "Redd, you have Winston Ashby and his wife both dead at his farm?"

"His wife is a coffin in the arena, and I feel certain Winston is in the other one. I didn't open it, wanted to reserve the scene.

I called the state police and ordered a team out and—"

"Okay, stop! Call the state back and stop them. I need to take this over."

Herring was surprised. "Why, what's this all about?"

"I'll fill you in later. Give me the details you have. Where they are, how you got there, whatever."

Herring started with the call from Kathryn and worked his way back to the coffins on the tracks and the one at the train station.

"Holy shit!" responded Berry. "Why didn't you tell us any of this?"

"What was there to tell? Until today we had nothing but mannequins in boxes. No link to Ashby, no link to anything."

"Oh Lord. There is a major link, and Ashby should have known it."

"How would we know that?! We never heard a word from him."

"We need to get to the bottom of this. I need you to stay there and keep everyone away from the site. I am sending a team. We will take the bodies to Richmond for autopsy and our team will examine the site. Go ahead and open the other coffin and make sure it is Ashby and call me back. That would be awkward if it's someone else in there. Call me right back."

Berry hung up and Herring went back into the barn, being as careful as possible to step in his first footprints with a minimum of new disturbance to the site. He opened the second coffin. It was indeed Ashby, bagged and wrapped like his wife. He replaced the lid and called Berry back to report.

Berry instructed Herring to wait at the farm, got directions, and hung up. He'd arrive with the team of investigators.

Herring used the waiting time to think over what had just happened. The haste and magnitude of the FBI reaction had

David Geiman

38

thrown him for a loop. Until now, he'd pretty much thought that the coffin episodes were twisted capers dreamed up locally. The hint of danger and threat had always been there but attached to nothing real. Now, it was a part of the narrative.

Ashby owned Celebration Farms and raised breeding stock called Celebration Angus. This much Herring knew from the papers and word around town. The farms had been bought by Ashby more than fifteen years ago when the former owner, a New Yorker, had gone to prison for participating in a Ponzi scheme. The scheme raised money to purchase prize cattle, expanding the herds faster than the market could bear, and faster than new chump investors could be sucked in. Cattle Ponzi schemes seemed to pop up once every decade or so and had begun in the US as far back as the late 1800s.

Ashby had previously lived in the close-by mansion that once belonged to a former DuPont general manager. When he moved to the six-thousand-square-foot main house on the primary farm, he stocked the two thousand acres with five hundred high quality Angus cows. He began a lucrative breeding business that produces and sells bulls for commercial farmers across the United States. It is reputed to be a highly sophisticated operation with genetic screening and artificial insemination. The commercial bulls are known to sell for ten thousand dollars apiece, and other select bulls used as donor studs could fetch as much as a half million. A far cry from the little family farm on which Herring had been raised.

Ashby was also an investor in an aircraft maintenance and renovation company near Winchester, eighty miles to the north. In addition to their commercial customers, the company did work for the government, so a security clearance was required to enter. Whatever they did for the government was top secret, but it involved twin-engine turboprop planes. Their camouflage paint jobs didn't keep them from being seen parked outside the hangars, and it was rumored that they were used for spying in the Middle East and in Afghanistan.

Ashby had been referred to as Colonel Ashby for as long as Herring could remember. He was frequently out of the country and was rumored to be invested in Indonesian oil exploration. He rarely mixed with the local people. Herring had no idea who his friends might have been. The colonel had a son who is a bit of a recluse and lives in the hills west of Staunton. He had worked in Europe for a computer company and is thought to be wealthy and eccentric. And he had a daughter who is unmarried, works on the farm and is seen in town from time to time. She is attractive but stern and rumored to be a lesbian, although no one knows who her partner might be.

Herring was unaware that Ashby's first wife had been unstable and had committed suicide about twenty years ago. Ashby had remarried around the time he bought the Celebration Farms. The new wife, Caroline, was from Williamsburg. She had been associated with fundraising at the College of William & Mary and still maintained an apartment near there. Herring had visited Williamsburg on several occasions. He found the old capitol attractive to look at but trapped in its past and not very interesting.

In spite of the litany of people, events, and activities that had just scrolled through his mind, Herring didn't know much of any of it to be fact. He hadn't investigated the suicide and wasn't even sure where it happened. He'd had no involvement with the investigation of the Ponzi scheme. That was FBI because of the multistate magnitude. He had met the one daughter but never talked with her. He didn't know the son or even his name and had never been in the airplane maintenance facility. A trove of half-assed semi-information is what he was, like the embodiment of a bad internet site.

Wrapped up in reporting to Berry, Herring had forgotten about Kathryn for a few minutes. He didn't know how to deal with her. She should probably not be allowed into this barn. She could be a suspect, depending on what the forensics team found. He didn't want to call her and tell what he had found. He didn't want her to come to the site. He couldn't leave the site to go and find her and report the news in person. He decided to wait until Berry arrived. If she called or showed up, he would handle it the best he knew how.

Part Two

The Killer

Ashby and Caroline descended the stairs of their plane and looked around. The hangar doors were slightly ajar, and they stepped inside. The killer emerged from the dark, pointed a gun at Ashby, and ordered them both to halt. The killer's message to them had been clear, and Ashby had discussed it with Caroline on the short flight back from the valley airport. They were both aggravated to have to return to the farm, but not overly concerned. This could be shut down quickly. Caroline was aggressive in all situations, be they social or otherwise. When she saw the gun in the killer's hand, she was more inclined to laugh than be frightened. This was not something that happened in real life. This was more like a movie thing.

She stepped up to the killer and reached out for the gun. The older model revolver did not have a safety. The killer attempted to turn the gun away from her, but when Caroline pulled on his arm the pistol fired. The bullet entered under her chin and penetrated up through her tongue and into her brain, killing her instantly. It missed the aorta at that angle and so the bleeding was minimal.

7

Asking Questions

True to his word, Berry and the team showed up at the farm in just under two hours and began taping off the entrances. Herring handed over the keys, and the team secured the airplane and the hangar. Kathryn had not shown back up, which struck Herring as strange, but perhaps she was actually ill. He and Berry decided to call her to report the findings and to question her. She sounded as if they woke her up. Berry wanted to see the main house, so they agreed to meet there in fifteen minutes. They told her they had information but would prefer to deliver it in person.

They could see the main house on a hill off to the southwest. They drove back out to the public road and turned left and drove about half a mile to the driveway. Pavement lights were mounted on both sides of the drive, and Herring thought they would light the way elegantly at night. The house was about two hundred yards ahead and had three flagpoles in front. An American flag in the middle, a Celebration Farms flag to the south, and what appeared to be a Virginia state flag on the north side. He was relieved to see there wasn't a confederate flag up on one of those poles.

It was a single-story with lots of glass and a slate roof and five or six chimneys. Built of stone and wood by talented craftsmen, it looked as if it would have high ceilings throughout. The driveway ended in a looping turnaround, with an apron that extended to a three-car attached garage. The surrounding landscape, with well-tended shrubs and flower beds, was bordered by a fence in the front. Herring guessed it all must have cost several million when it was built and would be much more today. Nothing else in the county could hold a candle to this place.

Herring had just pulled around behind the garage when Kathryn arrived in the black pickup. She looked more composed this time. Either she really had been quite sick or was good at faking it. Had it not been for the laugh lines at the corners of her eyes, Herring would take her for a no-nonsense person who was accustomed to being in charge. About five feet eight inches in height, she was fit and well-proportioned. Brown eyes, sun-bleached brown ponytail, classic features unspoiled by a nose that was a touch too big. She was wearing tight boot-cut jeans, a plaid western-style shirt, a vest, and stacked-heel cowboy boots. Easterners in boots frequently look ridiculous to Herring, but she looked as if she had been born to wear them.

Sheriff Herring reintroduced himself and introduced Berry. He asked if they could talk inside.

Kathryn motioned them to the door. "Did you find them?" she asked, almost as if she had hidden them herself and was wondering if she had been found out.

"Yes," said Herring, "but let's talk inside."

Kathryn frowned and opened the door.

They passed a sizable industrial-style kitchen before entering an expansive living room. Floor-to-ceiling windows graced at least forty feet of the far exterior wall. They framed a sweeping view across the valley to the fields and pasture below and on to the far hillside. Herring thought that in the evening you would probably get diffused light from the moon and stars. If he had been prone to looking at *Architectural Digest*, he would have recognized the furnishings from one advertisement or another.

Kathryn directed them to a conversation seating area, and Herring spoke first. "Miss Ashby, you called the office this afternoon. Would you mind repeating to Wendell here what you told Annie Laurie, our dispatcher?"

Kathryn looked at the sheriff and then at Berry. She seemed stressed but responded with confidence. "I told her that I had found the plane parked here when it should have been in Washington, and that my father and his wife were nowhere to be found. The same thing I told you when you arrived. Now you tell me what is going on. Did you find them? I assume so. Are they dead? Enough of the cloak and dagger stuff!"

Berry looked to Herring and then responded. "Yes, they are both dead. We found them in the arena barn. They appear to have been shot."

Kathryn put her hand to her throat, her mouth fell open in surprise. "Shot? Where? Here? Who?"

"We have no idea," said Berry. "I have a team down at the barns now. We will investigate the site and the hangar and the plane. The circumstances are a bit unusual. We will take their bodies to Richmond for the autopsy. But right now, I need to ask you a few questions if you don't mind."

"You can ask me all you want. But first, I'd like some explanations about why the FBI is here and what this is all about."

Berry hesitated. "Redd, I haven't had time to brief you on any of this. I apologize. We can talk later." He looked at Kathryn. "The death of your father and stepmother has the earmarks of a revenge killing by certain elements of the recent Middle Eastern conflicts."

Kathryn started to rise out of her chair, but Berry motioned her back down.

"Your father, through the aircraft business up the road, spent some time in some sensitive spots. He got his fingers into some sticky situations, which is as detailed as I can go now. We didn't know of any attempts being planned, obviously, or we would have warned him. But in light of what has happened, and with the information about the coffins that we just learned from the sheriff here, we think there is a pattern. We see enough of a relationship to past events that we need to examine everything."

"Relationship to what coffins? What the hell are you talking about?"

"Kathryn, sorry," said Herring. "We really need to back up and do this right. Have you seen any of the news stories about the coffins found in town, and on the railroad tracks over the past six weeks?"

"No, I was out of town part of last month at a conference. And I've been busy with a research class at school. I'm out of touch on local news. Fill me in."

Herring gave her the short version, then inquired, "Did Mr. Ashby, sorry, your father, mention getting any threats or warnings?"

"No. He never mentioned anything. Why do you think those coffins are related to this? Surely..." You could see the other shoe drop as she spoke. "Are you saying they are in coffins in the barn?"

"Yes, I'm afraid so," replied Berry.

"That is sick! You said Middle East. Which part? Afghanistan, Iraq, where? They weren't mutilated or anything were they?"

"To answer your last question first, as far as we know now, no, they were not mutilated. As to where the threats or attack may have come from? We can't say."

"Can't say or won't?"

"Can't, sorry. Have you seen anyone you didn't recognize snooping around or near the farm lately?"

"No, but I haven't been around the whole time. I help with chores and move animals sometimes. But this is a quiet time."

"Do you have employees? I assume you must."

"Yes, one full-time and one-part time right now. I can give you their names and phone numbers."

"Would they have been around this weekend?" asked Berry.

"Only in the morning to put out hay and check the pastures. It's been a mild fall so the cattle are still out on grass."

"Wouldn't one of them have seen the plane and reported it being here?" asked Herring. "Don't they check all the barns and buildings?"

"That's not really their job. The plane is frequently here. It wouldn't have been unusual to see it. And they don't know anything about my father's schedule. He comes and goes all the time. And there is no need to be in most of the barns at this time of year. The arena is only used at sale times."

"We will need to follow up on all of this," said Berry. "I know this is a bad time, but we need to secure your father's office or offices and do a search of the house for any personal and other papers. This has to start now. His plane and vehicles have been secured, but we still need his computers."

At this Kathryn balked. "You can have anything you want or need, but I need my cattle records. That's the heart of the farm and I use those every day. They have nothing to do with anything except the cattle."

"Miss Ashby, we'll have to be the judge of that. We can copy the contents and leave your workings undisturbed, but we have to get in as quickly as possible. I assume you have backups already?"

"Yes, but not to the cloud. We keep it on thumb drives in a safe. And the cattle business computer is not connected to the internet for security reasons. It is self-contained."

Herring broke in. "Wendell, can we leave some of this until tomorrow? I know time is of the essence, but I need you to bring me up to speed. More importantly, given what we have all just heard, with this Middle East business, do you think there is a danger to Miss Ashby?"

Berry rubbed his chin, and his eyes roved as he thought. "I wouldn't think there would be any danger to Miss Ashby."

"But you didn't think there was a threat to Mr. Ashby either. So how can you be sure?" questioned Kathryn.

"I understand your concern. But Winston had a specific involvement in what's going on here, and you don't. If you wish, we can provide some protection while we sort that out. Right now, we just need to get started. The faster we learn things, the faster we can reassure you. Fair enough?"

Kathryn looked intently at Berry and then at Herring. "That's a strange concept of fair, but yes, I guess it will have to do. I'm tired, let me show you where to start. I have the passwords for the computers. I already gave the sheriff the keys to everything."

If they were truly as concerned as they say, and Ashby had been as involved as it appeared, Herring wondered if the FBI's tech people had already been poking around.

"Are you staying here tonight? We can book you a hotel room in town if you would like."

"Why would I stay at a hotel? I have a house down the road I would prefer to stay in. But I don't know how safe that is. You tell me."

Berry turned to Herring. "We can have someone here to watch out for her tomorrow morning. Can your department or the state get someone out to sit on the place tonight?"

"I will take care of it. Miss Ashby, when you have shown Berry what he needs, I will follow you down to your house and wait until one of my deputies arrives."

8

The Federals

Through the night, the FBI agents searched the barns, main house, office, and the other out-buildings on the farm. A special team came in to look at the airplane. A forensics team worked over the hangar and the arena and took swabs and samples from all of the areas near where the bodies had been found. The plane was towed into the hangar, and the Ashby's luggage was removed and taken away for further examination. By Sunday morning they were finished. Herring had gone home to eat a bowl of canned soup and to catch some sleep. Blaine Wortham had taken the first watch at Kathryn's, and the state police had taken over at midnight.

Herring had slept fitfully, with continuous questions rolling through his dreams as well as his waking moments. None of it made sense to him. He had been in the military in a day and age when the enemy was fairly clearly identified. The revelations from Berry last night had shaken him. He had toyed with some ideas relating to the Middle East, googled some stuff. But he had never taken it seriously. Right here in this county?

Berry had provided Herring with a secure phone, and now it was ringing at seven thirty in the morning. The FBI team was finished with their work on the farm and would be leaving soon. Berry also told him he had the autopsy results. He told Herring he could share those with him, but not Kathryn at the moment. They agreed to meet at Herring's house.

Berry looked a bit worse for wear. Herring made him a cup of coffee in the Keurig he had come to rely on.

"Here's what we found on the computer. Not much so far. Everything seems to be related to the cattle business and the farm out there, or to his airplane. Not the airplane company, but the airplane he leases. It's a King Air, by the way, not some little single engine toy kind of thing, a model 250. This man had expensive taste. This is a three-to-five-million-dollar airplane. Don't know what it costs to lease it, but it's bound to be a lot. The cattle business must be better than I thought."

"This isn't your average sort of cattle business. When I was a kid," began Herring, "we would say that only doctors and dentists could invest in handsome farms with fancy cattle. It didn't matter whether they made money. Poor farmers had to somehow compete with that. But Ashby's operation is different. This is a genuine science- and genetics-based business. The appearance of the farm is part of the branding for the product. Would you buy a hundred-thousand-dollar bull from a guy with a beat-up pickup and a ramshackle barn? Not likely."

"Well, pretty farms aside, we didn't find anything. Other than the airplane being in the wrong place at the wrong time, and the Ashbys being found dead in some coffins in a cattle arena. We have a team working at Dominion Air Services up in Winchester right now. I will tell you what I can."

Herring took his time responding. "Wendell, I know you think this is some complicated international sort of spy thing."

Berry held up his hand to dismiss him, but Herring continued speaking. "There are so many holes in this and so many questions that we haven't even asked. I am having a hard time thinking this is what you think it is. I think you are implying that some thug or terrorists—and it would have taken a few of them to do this—just came in here and fiddled around with coffins and dummies and whatever else for two or more months before finally killing the Ashbys. And risked getting caught while putting them on a railroad track for Christ's sake, in a community where most people know most other people at least by sight. What was all that build up for? To scare the Ashbys or Winston, at least? We don't know if he ever saw any of it. And was it supposed to be a warning? If it was, I guess it didn't work. Unless you can give me something real and concrete and factual, I think I need to look at this as local."

"I understand your frustration. Let me tell you a bit more. But you have to keep it confidential."

"Wendell, if you want me to sign something to guarantee I'll keep the secrets, I am happy to do that. I signed some sort of clearance thing when I was in the army, and it is probably grandfathered. Just give me something to chew on here."

Berry relaxed slightly and nodded. "Okay, first the autopsy. They were both shot from the front, which is strange. Caroline was shot once from a low angle and the bullet entered under her chin and went into her brain and killed her instantly, we think. Ashby was shot twice in the chest almost straight on. The first bullet didn't do the job but the second one hit the heart. Interestingly neither body bled much due to the caliber of weapon. As you probably know, a shooting with a .22 is one of the few kinds of killings that resembles the neat and clean death scenes on TV cop shows. In real life, bodies usually have gaping holes and exploded heads and you name it. The .22 is instantaneous and foolproof and doesn't make a mess. In this case, there are powder burns on both victims. As you know, the bladder usually releases at death and sometimes the anal sphincter. But both bodies were undressed and cleaned. Then they were wrapped

in white cloth before going into the body bags. This is similar
to what Muslims do. They were rinsed with some sort of bleach
solution also, not sure why, maybe to mask smell. There was also
some salt in the body bags. Whether it got there by accident or
on purpose, not sure. But it did dry out and pucker some areas.

"The time of death was around four o'clock on Friday afternoon. They had been dead about twelve hours when you found
them. Rigor mortis was pretty complete by then. If death had
been later, the pathologist didn't think rigor would have been
fully established. Earlier, more advanced. Think about this. They
were most likely killed right after they landed back at the farm.
If what Kathryn says is true, someone lured them back here. We
need to find out who and how. We also need to know why. They
were either killed on the spot and taken away without leaving
any evidence or taken somewhere and killed and then cleaned
and put in the bags and boxed up, loaded into some kind of
van or something and then put in the barn. Then whoever did
it heads out of town. I don't think this could have been done by
one person. I think a minimum of two in this case. As you said,
it seems highly unlikely. Assuming at least two men, spread out
over two months, never being seen, never spilling the beans, just
to pick off two people in a really tidy manner. Think about it."

Herring responded. "That's my point. I can't see how they
pulled it off without ever being seen. And why drag it out? They
could have broken into the house, shot them both and been
gone long before we would ever have known."

"There is more, but I don't have time to tell you all of it
now. Just trust me for a bit on this and let me work on it. Our
team came in this morning to keep an eye on Miss Ashby. Go
over and meet them and talk with her and see what else she
says. Let me know anything more you find out. But I will just
tell you that I have enough background information to lend
credence to our hypothesis, however baffling."

"When will you release the bodies? And I assume Caroline Ashby had a family somewhere. Who is talking to them?"

"Yes, her parents are living in Florida. We sent someone down this morning. Kathryn has a brother. Can you coordinate with her to find him and tell him? I guess there will be some complicated will or estate plan for this many assets." Berry said his goodbyes and drove off.

Herring grabbed his hat and left to find Kathryn. He wasn't buying Berry's hypothesis.

9

Temple Grandin

Herring drove back to Celebration Farms again on Sunday. It was a crisp and sunny late November morning. Summer had been wet, and early fall had been unseasonably warm, and the autumn leaf colors had been spectacular. Several hard freezes had left most of the trees bare now, but the grass was still greener than normal. He recalled the days of his youth when November temperatures were colder. Some years there was snow as early as Thanksgiving. Now it was not unusual to have temperatures in the sixties in December. Two years ago, it had been eighty for a string of days in February and the co-op brought out spring greens and lettuces to plant. They were soon frozen.

When he got to the farms, he took the road to the north which led to Kathryn's house. The state trooper who had the morning shift was sitting on the porch with a cup of coffee. "Miss Ashby will be out in a minute. She's going over to the barn." He and Herring walked up to the door together.

"How is she this morning?"

"Good enough I guess, considering. What this all about? I was just told to keep an eye on her and not let any strangers approach. What's the mystery?" The trooper appeared to be in his late twenties, fit, neatly dressed. A slightly less square jaw and less imposing demeanor than a Hollywood talent scout would have cast. He seemed eager and was no doubt a rookie to have gotten a guard dog assignment.

"It's just a precaution because of the death of her parents and some confusion over the circumstances," explained Herring. "I don't think we'll have to do this for long."

The truth was Herring had no idea how long, or who was paying for it, or whether it was really even necessary. Out of his hands.

Kathryn appeared from around the side of the house, dressed in much the same manner as the night before with her ponytail pulled through the opening of a ball cap. Instead of the vest, she had on a lighter denim work jacket, stained with what looked like manure and grass. She carried a pair of work gloves in her left hand.

"Good morning, Mr. Herring," she said without smiling. "I need to go check on some heifers. I assume I am allowed to do that?"

"Good morning. It's Redd. I'm past the mister stuff. If that's okay, of course. How are you this morning? Are you over the mushrooms?"

"I'm better, yes, thanks for asking about it."

"I'd like to come along and talk to you a bit if I may. We can give our trooper friend here a break." Herring smiled at the trooper, noticing that his badge said Switzer.

"I would have to get authorization to permit that," Switzer said. "I will just follow along."

Herring asked Kathryn if he could ride along with her. She nodded but didn't speak. Once they were in the car Herring turned to her and said, "I want to say again how sorry I am for all that has happened to your family."

She looked straight ahead and said, "Thank you."

She turned left onto the road that led to the barns and sheds where they had been the evening before. To the right, Herring could see the paved landing strip which ran a long way down the edge of a flat meadow.

Almost a mile in, Kathryn drove past the first barns and pulled up in front of a horse stable. A half dozen horses were grazing in a paddock. When they saw the truck they perked up their ears and came trotting up to the fence.

"Normally I would ride one of the horses out to the heifer pasture, but since you are here, I think we should walk. Are you comfortable around cattle?" Kathryn inquired.

"I grew up on a farm. Yes, I am fine with them. Trooper Switzer, I think you should stay here though."

Switzer did not object, and Herring and Kathryn set off along a road that paralleled the runway.

"Can you tell me a little about how the farm runs and who does what? I need to ask you about some things from the last few days. But this morning I would just like to know a little about this whole operation. It is so different from my family experience."

Kathryn walked at a business-like pace, not responding. Herring let it rest. After a bit she said, "I don't know how much you want to know. Stop me when you are bored. This is my life. Most people don't know or care much about this sort of thing anymore.

"We have around five hundred mother cows here, divided into fifteen smaller herds for breeding purposes. That's thirty-three or thirty-four cows per herd which is what an average bull can service. We keep some pastured with bulls, and some are artificially inseminated. The numbers vary. We keep a separate herd of young bulls that are being raised for the sales."

They approached a fenced tract of pastureland, uncommonly green for this time of year.

"Do you know fescue, Mr. Herring? Sorry. Redd?"

"Of course. Tough in the summer and sweet after it freezes."

Kathryn smiled slightly. "Yes, it's a lovely fall grass when managed right. My girls love it."

As they reached the metal gate the heifers spotted them and came running. "I see you have them trained," said Herring.

This time Kathryn smiled broadly. "Yes, although I'm not sure trained is the right word. Do you know what low stress weaning is? Probably never had it in your day."

It occurred to Redd that "his day" was only twenty-five or so years ahead of hers, but he let it pass. And no, he had not heard of low stress weaning.

"We spend a lot of time with the mothers, both on horseback and on foot and with the dogs. Normally the dogs would be with me, but I had Woody come and get them. We spend part of most days walking among them and getting acquainted. Believe it or not they have personalities. When it comes to weaning the calves, we move them to a set of side-by-side pastures with a gate in the middle to connect them. I stand by the gate as they walk from pasture to pasture, so they are used to someone being there. I use the dogs to keep them in line and moving. We do this for a few days in a row. On weaning day, as we walk them along the fence, we direct the calves through the gate and into the adjoining pasture while keeping the cows moving along in the first one. In a matter of a few minutes in most cases, the calves are all on one side and the cows on the other. Then we close the gate. They can still see each other and smell each other through the fence, no trauma. In a day or so both moms and babies have moved away from the fence and don't miss each other. None of that desperate bawling and trying to get back together for days like it used to be. The cows are probably not unhappy to give up nursing a six- or seven-hundred-pound calf by that time."

Kathryn was clearly in her element. She seemed relaxed and almost happy as she shared her knowledge. The cows were clustered around the two of them in amphitheater style. Individual ones would ease over with noses extended to be touched, or to sniff at Kathryn particularly. But they were not skittish about Redd, and this was nothing like the behavior of the cows from his childhood.

"These are really nice heifers," said Redd. "So uniform, so calm."

"Yes, they are lovely. I love these girls. I like the cows, but we really raise a nice bunch of young girls here. They are like my children."

"No doubt this helps your reputation with buyers."

"To a great extent, yes. They buy for genetics, but our animals also handle well. Temple Grandin designed our working corrals. Do you know about her?"

He knew of her. She was an autistic savant whose study of animal husbandry and her own life experiences led her to develop a humane "squeeze box" animal chute. It was used to keep the cattle calm during inoculation and slaughter processes. As a scientist and academic, she was the first person to look at how cows and pigs see the world through different eyes. Most of the largest feeders and handlers of livestock in the US have used her services and facility designs. Herring remembered that he learned most of this from a recent documentary.

As Herring watched and listened to Kathryn Ashby, he began to feel a measure of respect for this woman. Her own compassion for these friendly beasts made him wonder if maybe she was touched by a degree of the same spectrum as Temple. They stood quietly while the young females paid them a visit and eventually turned away. Kathryn sighed. They turned without speaking and left the pasture, locking the gate behind them.

"I hate to break this spell," said Herring. "But I need to ask you a few things about when you came back to the farm. I'd like to know exactly what you saw and who else might have been around. And I need to talk to you about your brother. Is that right? You have a brother who lives somewhere near here?"

"Yes, well I don't know what else there is to tell about coming back early. I told all of you all of it yesterday. I came back due to being sick from a bad mushroom. Dad's plane was parked where it is now, and no one was around. I called your office, and you've been involved ever since."

"There wasn't anyone else around the farms yesterday? You'd think with all these valuable cattle you'd have someone here all of the time."

Kathryn laughed a little. "Sheriff, you of all people should know about the whole cattle rustling myth. It is a very over-blown impression. I mean, do you get many calls about cattle being stolen?"

"No, not a lot. Usually depends on the market at the time."

"Exactly. When cattle are very high priced there are individuals who will try their hand at it. But you need to have somewhere to sell them. All cattle have metal ear tags to show they have been vaccinated and there is a record attached to the owner, as you must know. If you take them to a sale barn with no tag, they won't accept them, and someone is going to notice. On top of that, our cattle have those tags, plus other special tags for our records and recognition, and finally they have chips, like dogs do, you know? And you couldn't just drive up and ask a cow to get in the back seat or jump up in the bed of a pickup. You would need some way to corral them and a trailer and some time. Pretty risky. We had one theft five years ago and the guys were caught in Roanoke within twelve hours."

"Okay, but still, on Friday while you were gone, and on Saturday and presumably this morning while you would still have been away, someone would have been here. Wouldn't they?"

"Yes, of course. We have the two regular cowboys I told you about yesterday. Woody and Bryan. I texted you their numbers. Woody was here. He and I inspected all of the cattle Friday morning before I left for Monterey. Bryan was supposed to come in and ride all the pastures yesterday, but he came down with the flu and called Woody to do it for him. Woody was done by noon, as usual. It has been so warm and so wet that we haven't had to feed hardly any hay yet, so choring is simple. This morning I called Woody and told him I was back and would ride the pastures, which I need to do now, if we are done."

Herring was slightly surprised that Kathryn had bounced back from the mushroom poisoning so quickly. He decided not to bring it up again unless she did first.

"I still need to talk about your brother," said Herring.

"He can wait. He's not going anywhere. He's out in the woods. Seriously. Let me do the pastures and then we can talk this afternoon. He hasn't been anywhere for five years. I don't think he will be leaving today."

Herring stood for a moment and looked at Kathryn. He was at least twenty years her senior, and he was investigating the death of her father and her stepmother. She was an unusual and unsocial woman who was rumored to be a lesbian. He felt a stirring of something more than just concern for the relative of a killing. Indeed she was probably high on the suspects list. But something in the way she had related to the heifers in the field, her genuine concern and care for them, had touched him.

Farmers were a disappearing breed, and people who worked closely with farm animals and understood them were few and far between. Pigs and chickens in buildings their entire lives, and cattle in feedlots for months before heading to the packing plants. Cows were even getting a bad rap for farting too much and warming the planet with methane. Kathryn was a very attractive and sexy throwback to a former era. In spite of her coldness, Herring detected a hint of vulnerability or sadness that had nothing to do with her father's death. He nodded okay.

They walked back to the barns together, and Kathryn excused herself to saddle a horse for the pasture inspection. He started to ask why she didn't use a four-wheeler but caught himself. That would have broken the animal/human connection that was so important to her work with the animals.

Trooper Switzer was still hanging around the barns, looking at the equipment parked there. Shiny green John Deere tractors, hay cutting and baling machines, funny-looking spiky-wheeled things that toss hay up in the air a few feet to dry it before baling. So different from forty or fifty years earlier when all of the hay was handled by hand and left on the field to dry.

Herring instructed Switzer to just shadow Kathryn at a distance. He hoped they would learn enough today to not have to watch over her.

Kathryn cantered across the runway to the pastures to the south of the main house. Herring watched as she approached a gate, unlocked the padlock at the top of a plate, the horse stepped sideways to allow her to pull the gate open, then walked through and turned to allow her to close and lock the gate. She headed across the pasture the way cowboys ride on the high plains of Wyoming.

10

Contrarian

Herring had left his SUV at Kathryn's house, so he had Trooper Switzer run him back over there, which took less than five minutes. He got to his office at about twelve thirty. It occurred to him that each of the discoveries of coffins as well as the murder itself had occurred on a weekend or within hours of one. He wondered if that was significant.

On Sundays, dispatch was forwarded to one of the deputies, so the building was mostly deserted. Herring sat down at his desk and pulled out a notepad. He had a growing mental list of things he needed to ask about or do. The younger deputies would pull out their cell phone and quickly tap in some notes. He preferred to write things down on a piece of paper. By the time he got through punching in the wrong letters with his awkward thumbs, the thought could be lost. Besides, he had read somewhere that actually writing things down helped you remember them. At least that was the belief when he was in school.

The first priority would be to get an update from Berry, assuming the crime hadn't been solved while he was out with Kathryn and the cows. Herring wanted to proceed with his own local investigation. He felt he might be more effective than the FBI.

To Do:
1. Go back to the farm and have Kathryn take him to interview the brother.
2. Check the barn and house for outdoor cameras.
3. Ask Kathryn again whether Ashby mentioned receiving any threats.
4. Establish that Kathryn really was camping. (How to do that?)
5. Research coffins, sand, rocks, gravel, salt, and mannequins??? (Talk to Wendell first.)

Timeline of events:
1. Saturday Oct 6, first coffin discovered on tracks.
2. Saturday Oct 22, second coffin discovered on tracks.
3. Saturday Nov 6, third coffin discovered by station.
4. Saturday Nov 20, fourth coffins found in barn with real bodies this time.

He wondered if there could be any significance to that spacing. The murders complicated things. He wondered if there had been a hired assassin. Were the first three coffins designed as a warning to Ashby? Nothing had pointed to anyone in particular, unless the dummies, the photos of the eyes, and the staging had some prior significance to the targeted individual. A meaning so exclusive that no one else would recognize or understand it.

More relevant, if they had been warnings, how had they been transmitted to Ashby? He had not been to any of the scenes. Thus, the culprits would have to have taken pictures of the setups and sent them to Ashby. The most direct way would be a text message or email. He would ask Wendell if they had found anything like that on Ashby's laptop or cell phone. Maybe there had been a written message to go along with it. But why not just send a threatening note saying we're coming to get you? It just occurred to Herring that maybe Ashby was being blackmailed!

Now that he thought about it, blackmail seemed like the most likely scenario. It could explain a lot about how something could go wrong, like a refusal to pay, and Ashby's subsequent death. It might explain why the plane came back to the farm instead of heading up to DC as planned.

Herring knew even less about Ashby than he'd thought. He certainly knew nothing about his involvement with the Winchester aircraft company. Nothing about his continued involvement with the planes themselves once they left the facility. Nothing about Ashby's actions and activities in the Middle East or elsewhere. He would have to let the FBI handle all of that. Indeed, it felt like the agency had taken the whole incident and wrapped it up in a cloak. As if they had made a decision that the deaths were an agency problem originating far outside of the farm and the county. He could only conclude that the FBI already knew much, much more than they were telling him. Otherwise the place would be crawling with investigators. If he had not known Berry for as long as he had, it's likely that he would have been shut out completely, ordered to not ask questions of anyone.

Being a contrarian, Herring needed more information to make sense out of the presentations of the coffins and the display of the bodies. The reasoning behind the timing, how and where it might have been organized, and who stood to benefit were all still unknowns to him. He'd worked in the valley long enough to know that the answers usually related to money, sex, drugs, and occasionally resentment or revenge. Criminal incidents were frequently fueled by alcohol and exacerbated by the arsenal of guns that continued to flood the area.

A new thought about the killings popped into his head. Maybe what the FBI knows would quash this possibility, but what if the target had been Caroline Ashby, and not Ashby himself? He knew nothing about Caroline or her family or about anything she had ever been involved with. Maybe everything was a smokescreen cleverly designed to hide the real target. That would open a can of worms.

Herring felt a headache coming on from the nights of disturbed sleep and concentrating on his notes. He could go for a sandwich about now, and the best French fries in the valley. He would stop by a funky little restaurant on Springhill Road called Mike's before heading back to see Kathryn. He wanted to go find her brother, and to learn more about her relationship with her father and stepmother. It suddenly came to him that during their morning chat she had not asked any more about how the two of them had been killed. Had Berry explained it to her in detail the night before? He thought not.

He glanced at Blaine's word-of-the-day calendar on his way out. *Prescient*, an adjective meaning having knowledge of things or events before they exist or happen. Having foresight. Herring had no way of knowing how appropriate that word would turn out to be for him.

Part Three

The Killer

When Caroline fell, the killer pulled back as Ashby, enraged and roaring, stepped forward to grab the gun. The killer's finger was still on the trigger and impulsively shot two more times. The first bullet entered Ashby's left lung beneath the heart. If Ashby had been wearing a heavy jacket, it is possible the bullet would not have traveled much beyond the surface of the skin. A .22 caliber, even at short range, do not have a lot of penetrating power, and will normally not cause even an exit wound. Because Ashby was wearing only a light shirt and sweater, the second bullet missed two ribs and lodged in the heart. With no heart to pump the blood, bleeding from the wound was minimal.

11

Surprises

By the time Herring got back to the farm it was nearly three. He had ended up eating a disappointing burger and fries at a fast-food place, forgetting that Mike's was closed on Sundays. It was getting chilly. The sun sets a little earlier behind the mountain chain not far to the west.

He drove straight to Kathryn's house and found a different trooper sitting in a different cruiser this time. He exchanged greetings, showed him his ID, and headed around to the back in the direction Kathryn had come from earlier in the day.

The house was situated about halfway down the slope of the valley on an upper shelf. Behind it was a gradual drop of several hundred feet. There was an incredible view sweeping over pastures and out to a woodland area and the foothills of the Alleghenies, and finally to the first ridges of the mountains. It was a lovely place to live, but Herring thought it would be cold in the winter with the winds whipping up between hills. Maybe that kept it cooler in summer.

The back of the house was sheltered by a privacy fence. The top of the fence was lattice, covered with neglected viny plants that grew up over and down the outside. He stepped through a gate into a flag-stone patio. Large pots of dormant plants lined the fence, and the cushions for the wrought iron chairs had evidently been stored for winter. The traditional brick house was painted white, but a recent addition running perpendicular to the back was sided with natural Pennsylvania lapped wood. The addition had a standing-seam metal roof that tastefully matched the roof of the original house. Double French doors stood open in spite of the chill. Kathryn sat at a table close to a fireplace that was set with logs, but had not been lit.

She stood up and invited him in. He noticed that she still had on boots and the jeans and shirt from the morning, so he did not ask about removing his work boots. He had put on his uniform out of habit before he left his house in the morning, but now it felt out-of-place, too formal.

She motioned to a wingback chair next to the fireplace. He sat facing a second set of open French doors across from the doors he'd come in through. Out that side was another enclosed flag-stone patio about half as large as the first. Like a room in the middle of a tiny park, the space was filled with light and felt warm and welcoming. He had never been in a room quite like this before.

"This is a lovely place you have here," he said to Kathryn, who had sat down across from him on a comfy-looking sofa.

"Thank you, my brother helped me design it. He understands things like materials, and he knew what I would like. Otherwise, I might have just left the house as it was, old and conventional. I'm very pleased with it and appreciate that he did it for me."

"Speaking of your brother, his name? Can we see him this afternoon? Have you called him?"

"Mr. Herring. Sorry again, Redd, let me tell you a little about Douglas, and then you will understand. Yes, we can go see him. But I think it will have to be tomorrow after chores. You don't just drive up to his house."

A puzzled look came across Herring's face. "You make him sound like a hermit."

Kathryn smiled slightly. "Yes, you might say that. But probably the world's wealthiest hermit since Howard Hughes. No, I exaggerate. Not that rich and not that crazy either. But rich. Let me explain."

This place and her family were full of surprises. An ex-military father with one of the most expensive herds of cattle in the country, who's a partner in some military spy business. And now a wealthy hermit brother living off somewhere in the woods?

"Douglas is a genius. I mean a certifiable genius. I don't know the exact number. His IQ is above 150. But along with his high IQ, he also inherited—or developed as is sometimes the case—something on the spectrum of autistic tendencies. Maybe Asperger's would more correctly describe it. He isn't much into people, but he loves numbers and design and abstractions.

"The reason he is rich is that he designed a lot of the components that go into computers and cell phones and the like. He worked for one of the chip manufacturers in Europe and they paid him literally millions of dollars over the years. And since he had no interest in people or an outside life, he saved it all and still has most of it."

Herring was taken aback. "So how come he quit working for these people if he was so successful and loved doing it?"

"Well, you would have to know Douglas to understand it. One day he says he came to the realization that what he was doing was evil, that it would lead to the end of human freedom and reason. He could not support that any longer. He also became more paranoid. He had always been a bit that way. He thinks that we are living in the end days, so to speak, with the financial markets on the verge of collapse and society along with it. His version of the end days does not include getting raptured up, if you are wondering. He is highly fearful of civil unrest and anarchic revolution, as he would put it."

"So where does he live now, in a bunker or something?"

"No, not exactly. He has a house, but it has some bunker-type elements. It will be easier to show you than tell you. But he has gone entirely off the grid in every way. No electricity except from his solar cells, no phone, no computer. No bank account, no credit cards, no health insurance."

"No bank account. Where is all of this money he earned? Under the bed?"

"No." Kathryn actually smiled at this. "It's been converted to gold."

"Gold. Gold?!"

"Yes, I don't know all of the details of where he keeps it. If something happens to him, there is a letter in a safe deposit box for me that will tell me how to access it. And I have to say, even that safe deposit box worries him. I don't know for sure. He doesn't trust most banks, but he may have some stored in Switzerland or Monaco or somewhere. And I don't know if he has coins or bars or what. Maybe he has some buried in the woods or in a safe. I don't know. He doesn't want to attract attention with it."

"Well, that is different," said Herring. "How does he function without a bank account and credit cards? It's harder and harder to pay cash. How does he get insurance for the house, or for his car? I assume he has a car?"

"Actually, he doesn't. I have one that he paid for, but it's in my name. As is his house and land. He doesn't want his name out there anywhere. He is very paranoid and is quite certain that we are months or years away from collapse as a society."

"So, how does he communicate if he doesn't have a computer or phone? I assume not even a land line?"

"Oh no, he couldn't get a land line in to where he lives. He comes by every week or two. He has to buy groceries. He has a larder and a stock of food that would probably last a year if it had to. He has his own water source. Everything to survive. If I vouch for you, he will show you."

"So what does he do all day? Doesn't a genius need to keep his mind stimulated? I assume he doesn't order books from Amazon if he doesn't have a credit card."

"That's not a problem. He reads constantly, goes for long hikes into the mountains almost every day. I order books for him. Plus newspapers. He writes articles and sends them out under a pseudonym from time to time. Predictions of collapse and warnings and so on. It all goes through me."

"Are you two close? You are the only person he ever talks to, right? Except for grocery store clerks or someone like that?"

"Yes, we are as close as his mental state allows. He is very concerned about me, very protective. He knows I could never live like he does, but I think he wishes I would."

Herring looked at Kathryn and shook his head. He could not conceive of a life without friends, even though he had fewer since his wife died. But he had daily conversations and links with dozens of people. Of course, he couldn't fathom how a computer chip was made either. Maybe that's part of the trade-off, but maybe not. Bill Gates could talk to people and was married and lived in a $120 million house out in public on a lake or something. Autism or Asperger's, Douglas was clearly one of a kind.

By now, the sun was close to setting. Herring would have enjoyed continuing his chat with Kathryn, but he needed to process what he had just heard. Not that he thought it had much bearing on the investigation. He was also still thinking about his morning with Kathryn, and her intense interest in and love for the cattle. Maybe love was too strong a word. Care was probably better. In one day, he had become acquainted with two seemingly strong individuals who fit no mold he had encountered to date.

There were a number of unanswered questions about Douglas, but those would have to wait until tomorrow. He wanted to call Berry and see if there were any updates on any of the items on the list he'd made. He bade Kathryn a good evening and headed home, secure in the thought that she was safe for the night.

12

Touchy

Herring was at the office by seven Monday morning. The first order of the day was to try again to reach Berry. He was curious if there was news that would impact his own investigations. He also wondered whether Berry's team wanted him officially involved at all. He had made up his mind to go back to the farm after lunch, and to try to meet with Douglas. He was pretty sure his interest in returning to the farm was related to the case.

Blaine and Roddie weren't in yet. He checked Blaine's word-of-the-day. *Extramundane,* meaning beyond our world or the material universe. Well, Winston and Caroline Ashby were certainly beyond our world now. And from what Kathryn had said, it sounds like Douglas is living in his own world.

By eight both deputies were in. Herring called them into the conference room and gave them as much of an update as he could. He asked them to pay particular attention to any unusual signs of activity around houses or buildings known to be empty. He had made that request six weeks ago after the second coffin was found, but so far nothing had been reported.

At eight fifteen his secure phone buzzed, and he excused himself and went into his office and closed the door.

"Wendell, good morning."

"Morning, how was the rest of your weekend?"

Herring filled him in on the basics of what he had done. "So, what do you have for me from the nation's capital, or wherever you are this morning?"

"Actually, a bit more than I expected. At least enough to know where to focus. I think this is going to stay in our laps."

"That seems like a big leap of faith or confidence of whatever," said Herring. "Did someone come in and confess?"

"No, no, nothing so dramatic. Settle down. Let me do this in order. You can take notes."

In spite of his generally cordial working relationship with Berry, Herring was a little irritated with him for establishing domain over the case in this way. He knew there were sheriffs who would gladly wash their hands of a case this ugly, but good ones wanted to be kept in the loop if something happened in their county and under their jurisdiction. Your duty was to keep your local people safe and bring them justice when that safety was compromised.

"Do I have to burn the notes and swallow the ashes when we are done?" asked Herring with a sarcastic edge.

Berry laughed. "Touchy this morning, touchy. Just listen. I think you'll understand. And then we can talk about next steps.

"Alright, first the results of the autopsy. I already told you how they were killed. And by the way, they were killed in the hangar. Our techs found minute blood stains. Someone had cleaned the floor and apparently tried to disinfect it, but the stains were found anyway. The killer must have picked up the shells. The bullets from revolvers, once lodged in the target, often become misshapen and unidentifiable. Investigators rely on the shells to identify the type of gun. But I'm not telling you anything you don't know. Our agents combed that area completely and found nothing related to the weapon. I already mentioned the cleaning of the bodies. That was most likely done in the hospital area for the cattle. There was evidence of human blood and the use of other chemicals.

"There was no evidence of rape of the wife. Both were in decent shape for their ages. Stomach contents showed they had eaten turkey and Swiss cheese sandwiches on a dark bread about four hours before death. No alcohol in the blood. Mr. Ashby's liver showed some sign of a lifetime of above-average alcohol intake, nothing to cause any problems in the near future. The bodies didn't show signs of a physical struggle before death. They were either surprised by the killer, who acted quickly, or they knew the killer and didn't expect this sort of action.

"There was no jewelry on the wife and no ring on the husband. But there was a band of lighter skin on the ring finger that showed he usually wore one. I guess Kathryn was not around when they left, but you might ask her if she knows what Caroline might have worn on such an occasion.

"There was one small thing that is still being analyzed. Winston Ashby had a small lesion on the brain that we are having looked at. It sounded from the initial observation that it could have either been the beginning of something, or nothing to be worried about. That's off for a biopsy. Either way it doesn't have a bearing on the case. It's not as if he was depressed because he had cancer or something and shot himself. Just an item to check out."

Herring was writing quickly to catch everything.

"Next, possessions. We found two suitcases for each of them on the King Air. Expensive clothes, fancier than the average tourist would wear. They must have been meeting someone important. Or maybe they just liked to dress up. A few designer labels for Mrs. Ashby, I guess not from Staunton.

And thousand-dollar suits and six-hundred-dollar blazers for Mr. Ashby. By the way, we have people who know this stuff. It's not in my wheelhouse."

Herring chuckled. The flow of information elevated his position, soothed his sense of irritation. Even if there was nothing to be done immediately, he thought all of this would come in handy at some point. The other coffins were still an enigma.

"Now, it gets more interesting. It looks like Ashby was flying the plane, and Mrs. Ashby was seated behind him but on the opposite side. Her purse was on the seat next to her. There was no briefcase, and no laptop on the plane, or up at the house. I don't know if you looked, but there are offices both up at the house and down at the barn by the hangar. Both have computers on the desks. The barn office was locked, but the key was with the ones Kathryn gave you. It's a pretty secure lock and a fireproof door. We took the computer, but it had only farm and cattle records on it. Nothing of a personal nature. We have copied everything we needed, and we will arrange to bring it back.

"The house office computer had lots more on it, emails and so forth, but nothing initially that sheds much light. We didn't find anything to suggest he had received an email warning about any of the boxes or anything else. He could have erased them, but we don't think they were ever there. I am guessing that his laptop would have had more interesting content, and possibly a different email address. There was some stuff from the aircraft company but most of it was tax related. We did discover that he had a lot of Limited Liability Companies and companies that owned other companies, all of which is pretty normal for a wealthy guy who wants to minimize exposure and tax liabilities. Our accounting people are poring through all of that now.

"So, on that front, we don't have much yet. But we did find a paper shredder by the desk and there were some shredded documents in the basket. It is a painstaking task, but we have people who can put some of this stuff back together. Fortunately for us, or for them, at least, there wasn't a lot of stuff in the basket. But it looks like there may be some photos from either the train station or from the tracks. We caught a big break there. His shredder is pretty basic and the shadings from both the tracks and the station are distinct on the strips. I am ninety-plus percent sure we will have something in a few days on that.

"I wonder where the photos came from, and whether he printed them out? Why would he have printed out stuff if it was dangerous to him? Or if it was evidence of something he didn't want out?" questioned Berry. "Maybe he was going to show it to someone? Ask for some help?"

"We need to wait and see what you come up with. They must have had a cleaning lady, and she would have emptied the trash. So the pictures must have come in quite recently," added Herring.

"Now, on to a couple of other items. Oh, I forgot. There was no cell phone in Mrs. Ashby's purse. But nothing else missing as far as we could tell. The usual credit cards. Amex Black card. I think you have to charge a million dollars a year or something to get one of those. Other Visa, MasterCard, and so on. Driver's license, insurance card, a little cash. Passport. Now, for the fun stuff. The Ashby's were booked in business class on the 8:00 p.m. United flight to London. There were other reservations a few days later from London. The fixed base operator up there at Dulles confirmed that Ashby's plane was due to arrive around 4:00 p.m. and was booked to be held at Dulles for two weeks.

"That's four hours to go from the FBO to the terminal. That's a lot of extra time, especially if you are in business class. Because those people get a special lane to check in, and a special lane for security. You can easily get through in thirty or fewer minutes, and certainly no more than an hour. Of course, for international you need to be on the plane thirty minutes before departure, but that is still way too much extra time. So, we think maybe he was meeting someone at the airport or nearby before leaving. Maybe at a hotel, who knows? We are checking."

"So lots of loose ends," said Herring.

"You don't know the half. Here is the interesting part. At 4:36, which is probably close to the time the Ashby's were killed, someone went to the United website and cancelled their reservations for the London flight. Someone knew their travel plans and the passwords to get into their United account. And whoever that is knew they were either dead or about to be."

Part Four

The Killer

The killer, rattled and surprised by the turn of events, reasoned that making it look like something it wasn't was the best outcome for the moment. The gun had to be hidden. The bodies would just have to stay where they were in the hangar. The killer looked out and saw no one around, as expected. The next step was to get in the vehicle, drive out, and hide the gun somewhere no one would think to look.

The killer knew of a place that was seldom locked. Step inside, make way to the room, and put the gun in a cabinet. As the killer opened the cabinet door, the sound of footsteps could be heard in the hall heading that way.

13

Nasty Stuff

Just as Berry was finishing his report to Herring, he was interrupted by someone in the background and told Herring he would call back shortly.

Berry's last statement had left Herring speechless. It meant that this had to be a complex, multi-person plot. There must have been individuals on the ground on or near the farm, and someone somewhere manning a computer. These were people who knew of the Ashby's plans to go to Europe. They had gotten hold of passwords or account numbers and knew exact flight times and how to cancel the reservations. Of course, most people don't protect their passwords well enough, and it would be easy to find the flight information on Mrs. Ashby's phone. They could have cancelled the reservations immediately after killing her. But that left too much to chance. They had known how they would handle it from the beginning. It was another taunting layer to add to the weeks of unexplained boxes.

The King Air had been in the shop for servicing at the Shenandoah Valley Airport. Winston and Caroline drove there to pick it up and fly it to Dulles. How did the killers get them to delay leaving for Dulles and fly back to the farm they had just driven away from? Why hadn't they just killed them at the house before they left? Presumably someone called them under the pretext of an emergency. Finding the cell phone records would be paramount. Or maybe Ashby had planned to fly back to the farm all along for some reason. But then Caroline would not have needed to drive with him to pick up the plane. And their luggage would not necessarily have been on the plane already.

A half hour later, Berry called Herring again.

"Have you found Ashby's car at the airport?" was Herring's first question.

"Yes, and we have it in DC. There was nothing in it of interest so far, but they are still going over it. There were no tracking devices, no fingerprints other than the Ashbys', and no briefcase or cell phone. I forgot to ask, but there must not have been any content on the memory of the car phone or they would have said."

"Well, all of this is interesting, but I am not sure I see why it rules out a local connection. Why do you feel it is all firmly in your lap now?" inquired Herring.

"I understand. Let me enlighten you. There is a small domestic section of the CIA called Protective Services, that provides security for certain threatened individuals who fall into certain categories. A federal judge who has been threatened, say, or a whistleblower or other government official who falls outside the normal Secret Service protection umbrella. In the last year or two, they have been unusually busy protecting whistleblowers. Also a few others who have been reporting on things they see in the current administration. Once someone's identity is known, and even in some cases when it isn't, this branch provides protection. Everything from bodyguards to safe houses and secure hotel rooms. Crazy but true. If you tattle in today's world, evidently people will be lined up to harass or kill you. Seriously."

"Lord, it's come to that?" bemoaned Herring.

"For sure. Nasty stuff. Anyway, around the time you became aware of the first coffin on the tracks, this arm of the agency got a warning. I don't know the full nature of it. It stated that an American citizen with ties to the Middle East, was on a list that an offshoot of ISIS had an interest in. No mention of a name, and at first blush not enough detail to take seriously. But this warning apparently came in from an uncommon source, not your usual nut job.

"No connection to a coffin at the time. Keep in mind, this is all after the fact. I don't know if you know this or not, but all of the information needed to stop the 9/11 attacks was out there prior to the attack. If traced, it would have led you to the perpetrators. The problem was that the clues were all mixed up with hundreds or even thousands of warnings and messages that led nowhere.

"So, to carry on, we are sort of in the same place now. After the fact. Someone was sending some little warnings that something was going to happen. The second notice referred to a reconnaissance, and the devils who design devices, and had some vague coordinates. The third message, two weeks before the killing, mentioned a Virginia company and a Virginia farmer that had got rich off of the blood of the martyrs, or something like that.

"It's too much of a coincidence to say all of the clues would happen to tie to this set of killings. Our job now is to learn more about what Ashby did to attract this level of hatred, and this desire for revenge. And why do the killings at his home? He travels all the time. It seems they could have killed him anywhere. Anyway, there are lots of questions. I think you can see why it falls to us to sort this out."

Herring was having trouble taking it all in. In spite of his history on the job, he had not become jaded or ambivalent about violent acts. With all that he had read and seen over the years, he still found it hard to comprehend that people could harbor so much hatred as this. And he found it hard to believe that some splinter group would have the resources to come all the way to the US just to kill a couple of people. It would make more sense to him if this was part of some larger effort, if there were more people to be targeted, or who had been targeted and killed.

"Okay, Wendell, what do you want from us? First, have Caroline's parents been told? Second, when can Kathryn and her brother have the bodies for burial or cremation or whatever?"

"On Caroline's parents, they will be told sometime this afternoon. They've been out on a friend's boat, and we just now located them. Once we talk to them, we can connect with Kathryn, and they can connect with each other. We will stay involved until they are in the ground or cremated though. Normal procedure in a case like this. And Redd? Please remember our discussion from yesterday. Nothing about any of this to anyone. You can investigate it like it's a local thing if you like. That might actually be beneficial depending on who is watching. Oh! And one more thing. I am going to keep someone on the Ashby daughter for a few more days until I feel like we have a clearer picture. I don't think she would be a target, but I am not sure why Mrs. Ashby was either. Maybe collateral damage, so to speak."

Herring hung up.

14

Kathryn

Monday lunch, Mike's on Springhill Road would be open today. Herring left the office after the unsatisfying conversation with Berry. He took a slight detour around town and picked up a sandwich to eat on the way back to the farm. He skipped the fries but regretted it. Mostly cloudy skies had given way to mostly sunny. A light chilly breeze out of the north made the day feel more like early winter than late fall, but the grass was still green. Herring had read that the rolling and repeating mountain ranges to the west of them made accurate weather reporting very difficult for this part of the Shenandoah Valley. The big picture, in terms of macro flows and trends, was relatively accurate. But conditions community by community were much more difficult to forecast. Unlike a flat state like Kansas, where a progression of thunderstorms was likely to affect a whole swath of communities equally, here in the valley one town could get an inch of rain and one a mile away would get nothing.

Kathryn's pickup was not in her driveway, but a few minutes later she arrived, trailed by a state trooper. Herring had arranged with the local state police office to be her guard for the afternoon.

She came up to his window. "I would prefer to take my truck this afternoon. I don't want any locals seeing your vehicle and wondering about Douglas. You okay with that?"

"Sure, I don't see a problem." Normally he would have insisted on taking his SUV as it held his weapons and a powerful radio and a computer link. But this occasion didn't seem to call for any of that. He would have two phones and would carry a portable two-way radio with him. Depending how far out into the mountains they were going, there wouldn't be any reception anyway. He had previously put in a request for a satellite radio that would work anywhere, but it was in the budget for next year.

"Have you eaten?" he asked. "I should have thought to call you and ask about bringing a sandwich along. I apologize."

Kathryn actually smiled at this. "Mr. Herring—Redd—I am not accustomed to anyone thinking about my food and needs. I have something in the fridge ready to go. Do you need a bottle of water?"

Herring blushed slightly. He was also not used to anyone thinking about his needs since his wife had died three years earlier. But he was a little embarrassed at not calling to ask if she wanted something from Mike's. Then again, he wouldn't have ordinarily done that in an investigation, so why did he feel a little guilty now?

She was back in a few minutes with a clean jacket over her arm. She was still wearing jeans and a plaid shirt and had a bandana tied around her neck to keep the cold air off while riding horseback. He had seen pictures of the cowboys who worked the pens in the feedlots in the high plains, and they frequently wore bandanas in the same way.

He buckled himself into the passenger side of the pickup. It was a cab-and-a-half but not a big fancy thing like so many people drive unnecessarily these days.

"It will take us about an hour and a half to get there," she said. "He is in a little valley just beyond Monterey. Back of beyond, but that's what he likes."

"So, how long has he lived out there?"

"Oh, I think about eight years now. I'd have to look at the calendar. He looked for a long time before he made up his mind. He had a lot of requirements. Didn't want any neighbors nearby. Wanted at least five hundred acres with hills and a stream. Wanted trees that would be good for firewood. He didn't want a road that anyone else would use, but he wanted to be able to get out when he wanted. Just accessible enough to be able to build his house, but then no one coming in to visit. Lots of boxes to check. Actually, I don't know if even this place would suit his standards now. He's even more paranoid and suspicious than he was when we found it eight or nine years ago."

"Where had he lived before this?"

"Ireland, mostly. He went to the continent occasionally, but he lived in a little house outside of Dublin."

"He worked in Ireland? I didn't know computer companies had offices in Ireland. I thought they were all in Silicon Valley or Washington State."

"No, no. I think it has something to do with the tax laws. He might tell you. Besides, with computers and the internet, people in tech can really work anywhere."

"Yes of course," agreed Herring. He could manage emails and searches and use most of the functions on his cell phone, but how the technology works was over his head.

"Listen, can we change the subject for a bit? Can you tell me anything more about my father and Caroline? Did you find out anything this morning?" Herring was relieved that she asked. He had had concerns. She had not pushed him for information the prior morning and that seemed callous and strangely distant.

"I'll tell you what a can. I have nothing that sheds any real light on who killed them or why. As we told you the first night, they were shot, with a small caliber pistol. Why they were in the coffins and in the arena? No idea. Obviously with the series of coffins, and their bodies in coffins, there is some ritual at play. No idea what that is. Your father's briefcase, laptop if he had one, and cell phone are missing, as is Caroline's cell phone. Otherwise their luggage was still on the plane."

He did not mention the shredded papers found in the office, the fact that someone had cancelled their plane reservations, or anything about the messages found by the CIA group. "Your father's wedding ring was missing as well as any jewelry your stepmom might have been wearing. Wendell wanted me to ask you if you had any idea what she might have been wearing on such an occasion."

Kathryn thought for a moment. "I really don't know. Since they were headed to Europe and would have been going through security, she probably wouldn't have worn a bunch of stuff. She always fretted about her bag being searched and people stealing her things. She was quite a pain about it. She probably would have had jewelry in her carry-on. They always flew first or business so they could sleep on the plane. You wouldn't want a lot of necklaces and so on for that."

Herring hadn't flown anywhere for a while and had walked through first class but never been seated there.

"Well, I guess there's an obvious question. How did you get along with your father and with Caroline? You worked with your father, right? With the cattle and the business?"

"Redd, I don't want you to get the wrong idea, but I was no longer very close to my father. I can tell you about that some other time maybe, but for now, let's just say we got along as business associates but not as friends. Anyway, most people aren't friends with their parents, are they? Douglas used to say you didn't need to like your parents, you just had to outlast them. I guess we did, but not in a very happy way."

"Alright, I'm confused. How could you and your dad run this multi-million-dollar business and not like each other?"

"Well, first of all, you need to understand that my father didn't run much of the cattle business. He used to, but I am really the key to it. He has the money, but I have the knowledge. I have a doctorate in animal genetics from Edinburgh University in Scotland. It's the premier school of its kind in the world. Celebration Farms Angus are my creation."

Herring looked at her in a new light. Amazing. This seemingly closed-down, lovely woman with such an affinity for a bunch of cows, a kinship that felt almost peasant-like, was a geneticist?! He felt like an idiot, like he should have been asking a lot more questions a lot sooner.

"So, if you and your father don't particularly get along, why are you in business together?"

"Oh, it hasn't always been this way. It would take a lot of telling, but things were better before Caroline. Douglas and I use the old joke about BC and AC, 'Before Caroline' and 'After Caroline.' BC was a lot better. Fortunately Caroline doesn't know anything about cattle, so she never got in the way of that part of the business. Frankly, not to be too catty, I'm not sure what she knows about anything. Her family is one of those multi-generational, old eastern Virginia families who can trace their roots back to the time the first one got off of some boat. And unfortunately they remember all of their names and like to tell you about them whenever they have a chance. They probably even know their corset sizes."

Herring laughed. It was the first light or humorous thing Kathryn had said since he had met her.

"I didn't know you had a sense of humor," said Herring, wishing he could take it back immediately.

Kathryn didn't seem to take it as an insult. "Redd, there isn't much you *do* know about me."

If possible, Redd thought, *I really should think before speaking.*

"Anyway, her family is very right wing, would probably still own slaves if they could. We had to keep Caroline away from the employees. She is very disdainful of those without a pedigree. I really pissed her off one time by suggesting we should have her family tree on the computer with all of our cattle pedigrees. She threw a vase of flowers at me. We haven't spent much time in each other's company since then. I use the servant entrance up at the house to get to the office."

"Well, I hope you didn't hate her enough to kill her," said Herring mostly in jest.

"Hardly. I shouldn't have spoken so flippantly. I'm sorry. I'm sad father is dead and sorry for her. She should not have died that way."

"Who is going to inherit all of this now? I assume you must know."

"I don't know all of the details, but it is set up to be mine to use but not really own. Something about generation skipping. It's in an estate that lets me live here and operate it until I die. Then it gets administered by the trust and the money goes to VMI or somewhere that father designated. That way we skip inheritance taxes, or most of them, and keep the place running."

"So that's how all of that works. It's why rich people never stop being rich. They just keep shoveling all of it downhill. But what about Caroline? Did she have kids before marrying your father, or other relatives who might come in for something on her death? Her own money?"

"Father had a prenup. I never saw it, but he told me the basics when they were getting married. She was to get a yearly allowance, I forget how much, but she couldn't touch the core assets and there were no other bequests for any of her family.

That was if he died and she was still alive, of course. I guess the rest of the terms of the first trust all just carry on now. I need to see the attorneys for all of that."

By this time, they had been on the road for close to an hour, no longer in Herring's district. It is only thirty-three miles as the crow flies from Staunton to Monterey, but forty-three miles by road. Most of that was over three or four mountain passes with snaking roads that seldom let a vehicle go over forty-five miles an hour.

"You've only told me a little about Douglas," said Herring, "How do you think he will take the news of his father's death?"

"Redd, I mentioned earlier that sometime we might talk about father and us kids. I still don't want to get into that right now. But when we were growing up, Douglas could do nothing right in the eyes of father. I don't know the extent of it, but I think there was some physical abuse and there was certainly a lot of mental abuse. I don't think that's what made Douglas like he is today, but it didn't help. So, the short answer is that father and Douglas have not spoken in years. I doubt he has much emotional connection remaining. I don't think he will have much of a reaction. He lives in a world of abstractions."

"Well, I'd like to say that's hard to believe. But I have seen some pretty awful stuff in my time as sheriff. The cruel and abusive things families are capable of is astounding. But you said he lives in a world of abstractions. What does that mean?"

"It's not that difficult to grasp. Computer software is an abstraction at most levels. You can't see it, but it makes computers function. You can't see the web or the satellite signals."

They descended the last ridge approaching the town of Monterey in Highland County. Most of the time it was a tiny insular village, a forty-three-mile drive from a supermarket. But twice a year it became a popular tourist attraction. Thousands visit for a few days during the spring Maple Syrup festival. And thousands more pass through when fall colors are at their peak. A strange area for Douglas to have chosen, but maybe everyone here enjoyed isolation, and he was just another secretive individual best left alone.

They drove straight through town on 250 and continued on for another five miles or so before making a left onto a county road that ran down into a narrow valley, alongside a robust stream.

After about fifteen miles, Kathryn slowed and turned off to the right on a one-lane graveled road. Five hundred feet further, they came to a gatepost that looked like one of the forest service access points that allow firefighters or forest rangers in but keep the public out. There was a piece of old railroad rail set in concrete on each side of the road and a high tensile chain strung between them. The chain was welded to one of the posts and secured to a welded ring on the other with a large combination lock. Kathryn got out of the truck and spun the dials to unlock the gate and dropped the chain to the ground so the truck could pass over it. Then she locked it back and they drove on. Herring wondered why she would ever have worried about locals seeing his SUV, given the isolation of this location.

They rode quietly and began to climb a mountain ridge above a narrow valley. About halfway up the ridge, they came to a parking and turnaround area with a one-car garage. It was a small steel structure, but the siding was much thicker than any Herring had ever seen on a residential garage. And the roll-down door was also heavy-duty, like the industrial kind that warehouses use for their loading bays.

Before he could say anything, Kathryn spoke. "This, and the entry gate are the beginning indications of Douglas's paranoia. He keeps his pickup in here. It's not like this one we're in. His is fifteen years old and has none of the computer electronics or built-in navigation or even a radio. He believes all of these things are just ways for the government to track and record where we are, so he doesn't want them. It's ironic in a way, because the government really doesn't need to track him anywhere, even if it wanted to. He hardly ever leaves here except to come over and see me every couple of weeks and pick up a few groceries."

"I guess it's the principle of the thing," said Herring.

"Yes, I suppose so. Well, we walk from here."

It was obvious once they got out of the truck that the ridge they were on now was man-made. The ground leveled out after a few hundred feet. They walked on what looked to have once been a roadway, that was now planted with saplings. Boulders had been strategically placed that made it impossible for a vehicle to pass. When Herring stopped to look at one of the stones, Kathryn spoke. "In case you are wondering, which I can see you are, this was the temporary road he had dozed in to build the house. When the house was done, he had the road roughed up and boulders moved into place to make it impassable. It would take a tank or a large bulldozer to get through here now."

Herring didn't know what to think.

They had walked less than a mile when the trees began thinning out. The outline of a cabin came into view. Herring could see a stone chimney, and a fenced-in area that looked like a kitchen garden. The house had a metal roof, and as they got closer, he could see that the side of the roof facing off to the south and slightly west was covered with solar panels.

An area of three quarters of an acre or so had been cleared around the house to allow the sun's rays to reach the panels. About five hundred feet beyond the house, the mountain began to rise again to the northwest. That meant the house was somewhat tucked into a southeast mini-plateau. It felt pleasantly snug and protected. Herring couldn't decide whether that was in spite of, or because of, the isolation.

There was no one around. Kathryn went up to the door and knocked. She tried to open it but it didn't move. "We will have to wait. He's probably out walking. I don't have a way to let him know when I am coming, so I just show up. Let's sit in the sun on the other side."

Herring peeked in the windows, which were small on that side of the house. He couldn't make out anything on the inside. The only sounds were the occasional blue jays complaining over in a set of low bushes, and some squirrels and chipmunks shuffling in the leaves. As they went around the house, the windows facing south were larger, but it was still too dark to see much detail in the house. Over by the southwest corner, there was a kind of drying rack with swatches and streamers of cut cloth waving gently and drying in the sun.

"What do we have here?" asked Herring.

"Ah, well, I was going to let Douglas explain it, but I can give you a little background until he gets back. Douglas is a quilter."

Herring stared at her. "A quilter? Like the Amish and the Mennonites?"

"Well, lots of people do quilting these days, but yes, it's the same concept. Douglas has taken it to a new level."

Any level of quilting for a male seemed like it would be a new level to Herring. "So, what is the difference between Amish quilting and Douglas quilting?"

"Where to start? You remember how I mentioned abstractions earlier. Well, quilting is quite tied up with math. Some forms of quilts are built purely on mathematical principles. There are even a few schools that use quilting to teach math concepts to people who can get it, especially the principles of geometry."

"You're kidding."

"Absolutely not. You ever look at a quilt closely? Many, uh, maybe most of them are made up of triangles and squares and rectangles and interlinking shapes and some stars and so on. There are some modern quilts that incorporate vision tricks, so they look 3-D like Heckler cubes. And some do Escher kinds of things where they create dimensions that conflict and fool the eye. You know who Escher is?"

"I've heard the name, but I can't say I know much more than that. My wife was the cultural one in the family."

Kathryn laughed. "Well anyway, there are probably hundreds of quilt designs. Some old quilts were called crazy quilts because once the basic structure was laid out, the pieces within the boxes on the quilt were irregular and didn't hold to strict geographic patterns. The quilt was square or rectangular and the edges were even, but you could do what you wanted in the squares. This actually made the most sense because quilts were made up of the ragged leftovers of worn-out clothes, so the piece sizes varied. I guess at some point someone with more of a sense of order, or an obsessive Amish lady, decided they needed to make them look more orderly. I'm sure there's more than one book about it somewhere."

"Okay. How do these multi-colored things drying here relate to Douglas and his quilts?"

"I told you he's near genius, and I guess most people with extremely high IQs need to keep their minds busy. He fears what he used to do, so he put his mind to work somewhere else. Did your cultured wife, as you referred to her, ever talk to you about art or the history of art?"

Herring grinned. "Not on a daily basis, no. But she did teach a little of it, and the teachers association sponsored charter flights to Europe and other places. So I *have* been out of the state of Virginia, and not just with the military."

"Don't go getting offended. I was just wondering whether you knew anything about impressionist painting. Vincent van Gogh for example."

"Oh sure. The starry night one. That was a popular song."

"Yes, yes, yes, of course. Did you and your wife ever go to the Musee D'Orsay in Paris on any of those trips you took? It's the one, by the river, that used to be a train station."

"Yeah, we did, I do remember that. I don't remember what we saw there though."

"Well, Douglas used to go there quite often when he lived in Ireland. And he became fascinated with the early impressionist work. If you look at early work, and at something called pointillism, you can see that the paintings are made up of tiny dabs of color and you usually have to stand back a bit to get the whole clear picture. I am sure Douglas wasn't the first person to figure this out, but he thought that these dabs were akin to pixels on a computer screen. You must have noticed pixels sometimes when you have a bad connection?"

"I am about as lost as I can be right now."

"Well, Douglas made the leap from pixels to impressionist paintings. He decided you could apply the same principles to quilting and substitute colored cloth for dabs of paint. Build up a painting on cloth!"

"Okay, don't hit me, but this is clearly not the velvet Elvis concept?"

"You must have real peasant roots. Why am I even trying?"

"No, no, go ahead. This is just not part of a normal day of law enforcement in the Shenandoah Valley. Now if you told me someone threw a bucket of paint on a boyfriend's new car because she saw him with another woman, that kind of artistry I'm familiar with. It's usually followed by a shooting."

"Alright, I'll quit talking. Short story long, Douglas developed this fondness for some of the pointillists and the impressionists and he has been making quilts of those paintings. He can show you, if he will. Someone named Cross is a favorite, Seurat. I don't know who else. Those rags blowing out there in the breeze are pieces of cloth he has dyed to get the right colors for the paintings. He can't always find colors he needs, so he dyes fabric to make it work. And in a six-by-eight-foot quilt there are around seven thousand pieces of cloth."

"Holy crap, seven thousand!" Herring almost blurted out something that popped into his mind but held it back in time. He was thinking that having to sew seven thousand pieces of cloth into a quilt would make anyone bonkers.

15

Douglas

"Well, here he comes," said Kathryn, as Herring was distractedly thinking about the seven thousand pieces of cloth.

Off to the north end of the clearing he saw a man approaching. He appeared to be a little under six feet tall and thin. He wore light brown slacks and a brown hiking shirt and an Australian style hat with a wider brim. As he got closer Herring could see sturdy lace-up hiking boots. He had a brisk stride. He glanced back and forth at Herring and Kathryn and began to smile, more it seemed for his own amusement than to express any particular joy at seeing the two of them.

"Hello, Douglas," shouted Kathryn, when he was still a little distance away.

He didn't speak at first but gave Kathryn a big hug. Holding his arm around her, he looked at Herring and said sarcastically, "Let me guess, my sister is here with a representative of the law enforcement arm of our government. That can only mean that something of some consequence has happened in the family. And since the only family that I have is sister here and a father figure, I'm guessing it involves the father figure? One of

Caroline's relatives challenge him to a duel for misbehaving at a Daughters of the Confederacy gala, and his pistol jammed? Or did a neighbor finally get irritated with his constant military references?"

"Douglas, stop it. This is serious. This is Sheriff Herring, from over in Augusta County. Redd, this is Douglas, my brother. Douglas, act human. Shake the sheriff's hand."

Douglas stepped forward and took Herring's hand. He had a firm grip. "Hello, Sheriff. So, tell me what's really going on here."

Herring glanced at Kathryn, who nodded. He realized that in all of their talks about family and quilting and art, they hadn't discussed who would tell Douglas about the deaths. It would fall to him. He decided to be a little pitiless and direct, to throw off the irreverent Douglas.

"Douglas, I am sorry to have to tell you that both your father and Caroline were killed sometime Friday afternoon. Shot with a pistol, and their bodies were placed in coffins and left in the sale arena at the farm."

Douglas looked directly at the sheriff, massaging his chin with this right hand as he pondered what he had just heard. "Well, that was certainly creative." He then glanced at Kathryn. "Sis, how are you doing with all of this?"

"I'm shocked, as you ought to be, at least a little, but I'm okay. The police are protecting me for the time being."

Douglas seemed taken aback by the last statement. "Protecting you? Why? Who thinks you might be in danger?"

Herring interjected. "Since it's such a strange set of circumstances, we really don't know if Kathryn is in danger or not. We don't know how it was done, or where. And there are indications that it might be tied to his work with the airplane business. If so, there could be contingent danger."

Douglas looked at Herring. "So I was right all along. The deep state finally got him. Or somebody's deep state."

"We don't know any such thing," responded Herring. "You could be in danger as well."

"Oh, I kind of doubt that. Father figure and I lived in two different realms. Other than depriving a few people of my brilliance, I don't think I caused enough harm for anyone to want to kill me."

Kathryn had moved away from Douglas as he spoke. "Douglas, I don't think Mr. Herring wants to get into a pissing contest with you right now. And it's really not about you. Can we just sit down for few minutes and act normal?"

"Sure, sure, sure. But I'm fairly certain, the good sheriff didn't drive out here just for the fun of it. Let's see. He must be dying to ask those sheriff questions. Uh… Where was I when they were killed? Do I know anyone who might want them dead? Do I have an alibi? Do I benefit from the killings? Answers? Here, lots of people most likely, no, and no. Asked and answered? Okay, now let's talk about you, Kathryn. How are the cows?"

Herring was somewhere between annoyed and fascinated by Douglas. He had not known what to expect from his discussions with Kathryn, and he had a preconceived notion that a person on the autistic spectrum would be less forthcoming, more closed down. But none of that was based on experience.

"Douglas, you are such an ass sometimes," said Kathryn. "Redd, what do you want to do?"

"Wait a minute," said Douglas. "Your real given name is Redd?"

"Reddford, yes."

"And your last name is Herring? Wow, Redd Herring. Someone had a sense of humor after all."

Douglas chuckled and then broke out laughing. "That puts a whole new light on things. Let's go in and have a cup of tea, and you can ask me questions and try to find holes in my alibi."

The house looked like a log cabin. As Herring entered with
Douglas and Kathryn, he realized that the walls were over a foot
thick. Douglas explained that the core of the wall was eight
inches of poured concrete with embedded reinforcing rods.
Wood siding like that of a log cabin covered the outside, and
the inside walls were framed and insulated, then finished with
either Sheetrock or wood paneling. The windows and doors
were normal high-end triple-paned units, but steel pull-down
shutters were mounted over the interior of each of the openings.
The house truly was a fortress.

Douglas opened one side of a set of French doors facing
slightly southwest, into a large great room about forty feet
long and twenty-five feet wide. A substantial counter divided
off the kitchen area. There was a heavy wood burning stove
toward the center of the back wall so that heat would spread
across the entire space.

The kitchen was a galley style with a short mini refriger-
ator under the counter. No microwave, no dishwasher, and
instead of a normal stove and oven, there was a wood cook stove.
Arranged beside it was a welded metal compartment holding
pine cones and kindling, small pine branches to get the fire
going, and finally a selection of oak and other hardwoods to
sustain the heat. The kitchen sink had one faucet, and below
the cabinet at the kick level was a foot pedal that would pump
water from a buried tank up through the faucet. A design
common to boats.

To the right of the kitchen was a hallway that appeared to
lead back to a bedroom.

Two comfortable armchairs and a sofa separated a conversation area from the eating area. The rest of the great room was
given over to a workspace with cloth strips and swaths hanging
in rows. There was a long narrow worktable with a partially
completed quilt spread across it. The walls of the room were

hung with quilts, several with normal geometric designs, and others with scenes from paintings like Kathryn had described in the car. They were truly stunning, even in the dim light coming in through the door.

"I told Redd about your quilting on the way over. He has been to the Musee D'Orsay, but he is not an art expert."

"Wow, that's a surprise," said Douglas facetiously. "What kind of tea would you like? I don't have anything stronger or more exotic."

"Just some water for me," said Herring. "Where do you get your water, by the way?"

"A spring up the hill. Pure and fresh and always cold. I have a little old-style spring house up there that also provides most of my refrigeration. This little thing here is just for bad weather days and two feet of snow." He nudged the mini with his toe.

"Tea," said Kathryn. "Whatever you are drinking."

Douglas had filled two cups with water from a clear jar sitting on the end of the counter where it would catch the sun's rays. It was already slightly warm. He put the end of a little device that looked like a soldering arm into one cup and pressed a button. Within thirty seconds the water was boiling. He repeated the process in the second cup, measured out some bulk tea into metal strainers, and set them in the water to steep.

Herring watched with fascination. It seemed like everything was designed for efficiency and to prevent waste. He couldn't see himself cooking on a wood stove or maintaining everything that made survival possible. Maybe he could do it if he had to. He could even see a little greenhouse dug into the hillside not far from the house.

"Where do you want to start? Heh?" Douglas mused. "Let's do alibi first. Since Kathryn has told you about the quilts, I'll show you what I was working on over the last week. Think that will stand up in court?"

He shook his tea strainer and headed over to the workspace.

"You probably never heard of him, but there was a post-impressionist painter named Henri-Edmond Cross whose technique involved the use of little dabs of color. But his dabs were a little bigger than some other artists. Say Seurat. Seurat must have been seriously intense since he probably had a hundred dabs for each one of Cross's. Let me show you."

Douglas went to a side table and pulled up two very clear photographs of two paintings. "Now look, here is the Cross piece I am working on right now. It's called *The Cypresses at Cagne*. Take this magnifying glass and look at any part of the painting. Oh, here, maybe a little light would help."

Douglas snapped on a lamp, and Herring took the glass and peered at the painting. Even though he had looked at the paintings on the walls in the museums, he had not focused on the detail. What he could see was indeed, hundreds or thousands of individual little dots of color. Some of them even looked like little loaves of bread or pieces of rolled and sewn cloth. At magnification, the painting had a quilt-like quality.

"That is amazing. It *is* like the little pixel things Kathryn mentioned on the way over."

"Yes, sure is. We don't need to get into any of that now. What I have done is calculate a quilt size that will permit me to use and sew onto the backing, the smallest color unit the artist painted. Fortunately, he was pretty consistent and most of his dots or blocks are the same size. That was the simple part of this piece. Color was another problem. I didn't like the colors I could find, so I'm dying strips to make the colors I need for this. I'm on a sort of parallel track with the impressionist paint-ers. They were able to create so many colors and get so creative and paint outdoors because of the invention of the paint tube in 1841. I think it was Renoir, whom you must have heard of, who said that if the paint tube hadn't been invented then, impressionist painting would not have been possible. An artist could mix up his own palette on the spot with tubes. Otherwise he had to grind up materials and mix them with oil and do a lot of prep for every color. I am making the same journey, just with cloth."

"But Kathryn says you never sell these. You just spend months or years making them and just hang them here or fold them away. Don't you want some recognition for all this work?"

"Ah jeez, here I thought there was hope for you. I don't think we have time to get into it today, but you come back some day and I will tell you what God and I have in common. I mean the old God, the Old Testament one. We both have worked with a certain level of frustration and disappointment. God supposedly created all of these beautiful mountains, and the rest of the incredible planet. And there wasn't anything around to see it that could appreciate it until sixty thousand years ago. I'll let you think on that."

"You going to have God testify that you were here over the weekend?" asked Herring, a bit miffed that Douglas was taking this all so lightly.

"Hey, send him a subpoena, and see if he shows up."

At this Kathryn, who had been following the discussion and watching for reactions decided to step in. "Redd, I think we need to leave now. Douglas is not going to say anything helpful, and you won't know any more in an hour than you do now. And he's not going anywhere. Unless you seriously think differently, I'd like to leave. We can come back in a day or two. Doug, will you come to the funeral when we have one? Do you care about the will? Do you care about any of it?"

Douglas put his arm around Kathryn like he had done out on the patio. He actually looked a little chastened, but not subdued. "Sis, I don't know about the funeral. If it would help you, maybe. I don't care about the rest. You should know that. I only care about you being safe." He paused. "You will have to come back with info about the funeral. I don't feel up to leaving here for a bit."

16

The Ride Back

In half an hour they were down the mountain, through the gate, and back on the road to Monterey and on to Staunton. Herring was frustrated that he hadn't learned much of substance relative to the killings, but he wasn't sure what he really expected to learn. Douglas didn't seem to be a likely candidate for the killings. It would have taken a lot of organization and trips down to Staunton to set up the warnings. And there was no workshop at his house for building coffins, and he supposedly had no phone and no computer, or at least not one with internet service. If he truly almost never left his mountain lair, the whole process would be out of character.

"I don't see how a person can stand that much isolation," said Herring, once they were in the car. "To go from working and living in Europe and working with other people on a daily basis to moving back here and living like the settlers did two hundred years ago? Is that part of his mental state or diagnosis or whatever?"

"Well I wouldn't say he's living like the settlers did, but yes. I think there are a lot of people in the tech or software fields who are on some spectrum like Douglas's. Well, maybe not a lot, but more than in other industries. When I visited him in Ireland, he lived alone in a little house out in the country. Most of his work was individual, and there was a liaison person who translated his work or merged it or however you want to say it. So he's always been more of a loner. Nothing like the sales and marketing people, or anyone who needed to meet the public."

"His comment that he and God both had disappointments to deal with? That was interesting."

"Oh, that's part of a whole set of conversations that's like a short history of the world. You will have to, well you don't have to, but if you *want* to, you can get the whole story the next time we are out here."

"A hint?"

"Okay, a while back Douglas told me that if he were God, or I guess if he had been God back in the early days, he would have committed suicide."

"That's a bizarre take on things."

"He says he thinks the book of Genesis should have been named *Nemesis* instead. His view is that Genesis was a predictor for how the world would turn out, and God should have just shut the whole thing down before there was too much damage. There are a couple of really phenomenally grotesque paintings in the D'Orsay that depict being driven from the Garden of Eden and civilization being ravaged by war and pestilence. Douglas used to go back and look at them over and over. I'm surprised he hasn't tried to make a quilt out of one of them. He says that if your first two kids can't stand to live in paradise, and your first two grandkids end up with one killing the other, there isn't much hope."

Herring shook his head. "If he really feels like that, what keeps him alive?"

"Oh, I think most of that talk is just cynicism. He likes the shock value. But he forgets that if he wants to shock people, he needs to talk to them."

"Do you think he is capable of killing someone? Of killing your father? And Caroline?"

"No, I can't conceive of it. He used to hunt and eat venison and ate meat from the store occasionally. But one day he told me he couldn't do it anymore. He said it felt like a betrayal of his friends. He was in the forests so much that he said the deer stopped being afraid of him and developed what he saw as trust. He said killing them was easy, but it was a betrayal of trust. He thinks betraying trust is the biggest sin there is, and he has a broad definition of trust. So he quit hunting and eating any kind of meat. He's a vegetarian now."

Herring looked at Kathryn and composed his thoughts. "Your brother is a very complicated person. I wonder what a psychologist would say?"

"Don't go there..."

"I'm not proposing it, just wondering. He is certainly a different dude."

"Redd, what is going to happen next? Are the FBI people going to take this over, or I guess they sort of have? How will they make a decision about me? I don't know what I feel. It's maybe naive and foolish but I don't really feel frightened. I haven't from the moment I came back and saw the plane, and father and Caroline weren't around. I was concerned for them, but not for me. I just don't see how I could fit in any of it."

"Well, Kathryn, I really, really hope that is true. I would not want to see any harm come to you."

Kathryn glanced at him and then directed her attention back to the road. They were just leaving the little town of Churchville and would turn off south to the farm shortly. "Redd, I've only known you for a couple of days, but I really appreciate you doing the things you are doing. And I appreciate you not flying off the handle at my brother. He can be really, exceptionally annoying. It's not entirely his fault, but it doesn't make it any easier to deal with him. It is the spectrum in part, but he's also a butt on his own terms sometimes. And I appreciate your concern for me."

Herring started to interrupt, but she held up her hand.

"No. I know this is your job and most of all you need to find out who killed my father and Caroline. But I think at base you are a good and kind person and you care about the people here. You are strangely very attractive for a man, in one way."

Herring stared at her with a puzzled look on his face.

"You actually listen when people talk."

17

Headache

Kathryn dropped Herring back at his vehicle at her house Monday evening. A new trooper had arrived to stand security until midnight when the shift would change. It was almost dark and she was headed back to the pasture to make a quick evening check on her heifers. Some of them were coming into heat and tended to ride and annoy other animals in the groups.

On Tuesday, Herring called into work. The dispatcher on duty had nothing urgent for him to look into. He decided to stay at home and call Berry from there. He needed a game plan for Kathryn's security and a game plan for himself.

Berry must have been expecting his call, because he answered on the first ring. "Morning, how was your Monday?" he asked. Herring gave him a quick, highly redacted version of the day, giving minimum time to the quilts and art and mainly expressing his doubts that Douglas was involved. He based his thinking on Douglas's hermit-like existence, the lack of any indication that he might have had the tools or equipment to deliver the boxes, and the lack of any motive.

"I expect you are right," said Berry. "I still don't have a lot of specific detail, but I have a background report on Ashby that I will email you shortly. It doesn't contain any state secrets, but keep it secure anyway. I do have some information that won't be in the report I am sending. It will make more sense when you have read the report, but here are some things that I think will be important.

"First, Ashby's military career was cut short after he became a colonel, due to some indications of unethical behavior. He may have been planning to leave the military by then anyway. Some of his associations may have created some conflicts of interest. Nothing was ever proven, but he was out. And that was when he became heavily involved in the airplane business.

"Now, in addition, there were unsubstantiated rumors that he had a cruel streak, and a few soldiers asked not to be assigned to him. More importantly, once he entered the civilian world in the airplane business, he went back to some of those same areas, particularly along the Turkish and Syrian borders. Even more to the point, he was there not long ago during some incident that I don't have details for. But I should know more tomorrow if I can wrestle the info out of the right people. I won't tease you with meaningless details now, but I think we may have something to chew on shortly."

Herring was about to interrupt, when Berry continued, "And, it appears that Ashby did have a photo of one of the coffins. It looks like maybe the third one, but our puzzle person is still trying to reassemble it. So Ashby was almost certainly threatened or warned."

"But no sign of the laptop or anything from it?" asked Herring.

"No, but boy would I love to have it. We have no links so far. If he backed it up, we can't find it. There is no link to the Cloud. His desktop in the home office is linked and backed up, but that is all business stuff. He seems to have done a very complete job of isolating business stuff from anything personal.

That is very disciplined and highly unusual. Even some of our political candidates who ought to know better, have not always been that careful."

"Okay, I think I have all of that. Now on the personal, have Caroline's parents been told?"

"Yes, they were met at the pier when they got in yesterday. We didn't want to have the Coast Guard go out and bring them in or say much on the radio, so we just waited once we knew where they were. It wasn't going to change anything for them anyway."

"Do you have a report on their reaction? Kathryn tells me they are very old-Virginia conservative."

"Apparently the father was quite stiff and excessively dignified about it, but the mother nearly collapsed. We have interviewed the father, and he has no knowledge of anything untoward, but he isn't fond of the farm or the area and they didn't visit there often. I get a sense that they think anything past Charlottesville is still the frontier, or at least not sophisticated enough to warrant a visit. The father—uh, what is his name? It's around here somewhere. Never mind—demanded the release of her body but was told we will need to hold onto them for another week or so. He was going to call his congress person or senator or the governor or someone. Maybe all of them."

"Well, that fits with what Kathryn said about them," said Herring. "Still, it can't be anything but awful to hear of your daughter's death, especially not her murder."

"No, you're right, but we have to deal with what we have here. I'm sure they would like to see the killer caught."

"So, anything else for now on that end?"

"No, I'll email you the background on Ashby."

"Now what do we do about protection for Kathryn?"

"I was going to get there in a minute. I want to get everyone on our team on a call, and the rest of the resources involved in this, and come to a group decision. My own judgment is that this is something that is the result of Ashby's bad actions in a war zone and he was targeted to send a message or for revenge. And I do have something to support that. You remember we talked about how unrealistic it would be for someone to come here from, say, Syria, or Iraq, or wherever, a couple of days ago?"

It was fresh on Herring's mind. "Yes, I still think that."

"Well, they wouldn't need to. After 9/11, the newly created Homeland Security department started looking into lots and lots of groups, known and unknown, in the US. And like any good card-carrying government agency, they came up with some initials for these groups. One of them is a segment they call DVEs or Domestic Violent Extremists, and the second group is called HVEs or Homegrown Violent Extremists. And both of these groups can be in touch with FTOs or Foreign Terrorist Organizations like ISIS. I am not making this up. You can find it on the Homeland Security website. I don't know what separates a DVE from an HVE since they both seem to be from home here, but through their intelligence networks, they have found that the HVEs in particular, I guess, are willing to carry out deeds for FTOs."

"I'm about to get a headache," said Herring.

"I understand, but in spite of all the initials, this is serious crap. And the upshot is that a group in Syria or Iraq, for example, could have co-opted a group in the US to carry out its wishes. Now, this ISIS group or whatever, is not going to send a note over to some group of pissed off wingnuts who have a grievance against this, that, or the other. They're not going to ask them to please go out and kill some former general because he tortured one of their cousins. What they *will* do is figure out something this general did that caused harm to a cause these wingnuts support. Maybe they tell these guys the general is secretly supporting Muslims, or screwing kids, or drinking their blood, or something equally bizarre. As long as it sounds legitimate so that the wingnuts don't think they're being messed with. And the FTO is not going to identify itself as The Sword of Allah or anything remotely alien to the wingnuts, but more likely as the Syrian Brotherhood of Persecuted Harley Owners for God, who knows."

"I sort of get what you're saying, but I don't recall a single arrest or a wanted notice coming across my desk as sheriff, that ever, ever pointed to such a thing."

Berry sighed. "Yes, I know, but there have been arrests, thwarted terrorist attacks over the years, and some of them do involve these combinations. We honestly don't know how many killings might also be linked to some of these groups. I don't know what your clearance rate is, but nationally 36 percent of murders never get solved. Now, very few of those fit this kind of pattern, but we do think a few come from these groups. There is an anomaly that doesn't help. You know in major incidents, like plane bombings and major attacks, every group out there claims credit. But with the Ashbys, it's the opposite. The perps don't want anyone to know who is behind it. So no one claims credit. Besides, if you kill someone in the US, the law *will* come after you, so you usually don't tell no matter what. It's not like you're living in some cave in the mountains of Afghanistan with a short-wave radio."

Being a sheriff, Herring knew some stuff about terrorist threats. He had more experience dealing with drugs, especially meth. He had supported a raid a little over a year ago when a drug dealer's minion had written down the wrong country road name and gone to the third house on the left of Tower Road instead of Flower Road, two miles away. He took a Mennonite farmer and his wife hostage while demanding they pay up the twenty thousand dollars in drug money he had been sent to collect. The family's daughter, coming back in from collecting eggs in the chicken house, overheard the threats and ran next door to get the neighbors to call the police. In this case, all ended well, with the Mennonites safe, the drug courier arrested, and a dealer arrested at the right house.

"This is all well and good, but at the moment, we don't have a local group, what did you call them, homegrown? Or even a foreign group identified. We just have some speculation that provides an explanation for an otherwise unexplained killing. When do I, or we, get something concrete?" asked Herring somewhat impatiently.

"We are working on it day and night, Redd, day and night." We are building up a picture and I hope I have enough in a day or so to see where a motive might lie. There is a specific incident that links Ashby, some bad actions, and a terrorist group, but I need more details. For that I am going to need some people to release some documents, or at least point us in the right direction. I actually feel pretty confident about this set of links."

"Well, Wendell, that is all we live for down here in the country, that highly confident stuff you guys generate."

"Screw you, buddy. You will get what I can give you when I can get it for you. I think Yogi Berra said that."

This caused both of them to laugh.

"Seriously, look at the report I have just emailed, and I hope to have enough by tomorrow morning, maybe sooner, to drop the security for Kathryn. I think that if they were going to do more than they have, they would have done it by now. Keep in mind the last two coffins each held a body, so I think they sent the message and then followed up. If I had to guess…"

"Go on?" said Herring.

"No, I won't," countered Berry, and he hung up.

18

Colonel Ashby

After he hung up from the call, Herring went to his desktop computer and pulled up a secure—more or less—site that was reserved for officers of the law. He downloaded the short report that Berry had sent.

Much of what was in the report relative to the military and the promotion process at least, Herring already knew. Ashby had been in ROTC in college at Virginia Tech and had moved through a series of positions. He majored in business and his early assignments had been in logistics and supply. He saw combat in the first Iraqi invasion as part of his requirement as an officer, but there were not details on the nature of his assignment.

If there were no disruptions or complaints, he would reach the rank of lieutenant colonel after sixteen years in the service. There is a cumulative 41 percent chance of making it to lieutenant colonel status in the service, and Ashby made it. His ratings were excellent, and his promotions came on time. The military has a very structured program for advancement. You are either up or out in the officer corps. And advancement is dependent on all A ratings by your superior officers. It would be another six years before Ashby would be eligible for promotion to colonel, and fewer than half of those at the lieutenant colonel rank would make it. He must have done well and kept an excellent record, because he made the rank of colonel in just over six and a half years, during the Clinton Administration.

Berry reported that there were restrictions on Ashby's records for the five years he spent in the Balkans. It was no wonder that those records were still classified. Clinton knew that Congress would not declare a state of war as the former Yugoslavia was falling apart. Ethnic cleansing spread across the area with some of the worst human rights violations since World War II. Instead, Clinton called on NATO to intervene with a bombing campaign, which was highly controversial and did not bring the Serbs to their knees.

More importantly, Clinton ended up using more private contractor services for on-the-ground action. These PSCs or Private Security Contractors, who flourished during the second Iraqi invasion under Bush the younger, were rumored to have gotten their starts in Bosnia-Herzegovina and in Serbia in the late 1990s. Details were sketchy and most of the documents were still classified, but Ashby had been in the region. It was there that he began to shift his interests to the private side of the military business, and where it was rumored that he may have discovered a taste for torture and brutalization. Berry did not cite sources, but he would not have written these things without having something to back them up.

Herring knew some of the history of the US military over the past three decades, but nothing detailed. He had been astounded at the use of mercenaries, for security and other functions during the Iraq invasion. He had heard that they are in use in Pakistan and other sensitive areas to this day. You normally thought of mercenaries as soldiers for hire in civil wars in Africa. For some reason Nigeria seemed to need them, and they had been involved in the civil war when the Igbo's tried to secede. A few had been hired in recent years to try to put down the Boko Haram group, but they had not succeeded.

Just as he was finishing the brief from Berry, his special phone rang again. He surprised to hear from Berry so soon. "What's up?"

"I just got off the phone with someone over at Homeland. They have been coordinating with army intelligence and the advocate general people. It's a mess because there is a civilian contractor involved, but basically here's what we have. It's sort of everyone in the wrong place at the wrong time. I'm telling you this in confidence. There won't be a follow up memo." Herring sighed. Normally this was the way you first spotted the line on which someone was about to hang your ass out to dry. He hoped that wasn't the case here.

"So, we already know Ashby is involved in this surveillance airplane thing. In fact, some of the planes they retrofit are these smaller King Airs and Gulfstreams. Propjets and so on. These days we usually think of spy planes as either drones, or U2s like the Russians shot down that fly up at seventy thousand feet or something similar. But except in active battle situations, a lot of surveillance is done a lot lower and a lot less sophisticated. Probably at twenty-five thousand feet or so. And most people don't know this, but it's almost impossible to shoot down a plane with a rifle. The bullets lose velocity by ten thousand feet, assuming you could even track the plane with your scope. And build in windage and speed and plane speed and the whole works. So, it's easier to do surveillance than you'd think. Anyway, Ashby gets to go out to the places where these planes are used, since he is part of the company that fits them up. I'm not sure what value he adds, but maybe he just likes playing soldier again without having to sleep in the barracks. Who knows?

"Now, a while back, dates not available, Ashby happens to be up near the Turkish border with some US troops when they get a report that one of the planes his company fitted with cameras has been hit and possibly crash-landed, in spite of what I just said. So maybe it was a mechanical failure, or maybe they were flying low and someone actually did get lucky. They jump on a chopper and head up a pass to the site where the plane had the issue. Sure enough, they locate it through a transponder on the downed plane. It turns out the plane had a semi-controlled landing on an abandoned railroad track, but then hit a gulch and flipped and broke apart. There are locals around the plane, but they run when they hear the chopper. When the chopper lands, the army guys and Ashby find one of the pilots dead from the impact. The other had survived the crash it seems but had been pulled out and killed by the locals. They had been stripping and cutting at him when the chopper appeared. This is all bad, but even worse is that Ashby knows the poor guy who was being cut up. He had worked with him in Winchester as part of the training for the operation of the cameras. And had flown with him in the valley on training missions."

Herring had been looking out the window at the sunlight on the Allegheny mountains as Berry spoke. The light on the pines and in the hollows seemed to shimmer. There were a few scattered clouds and the rolling shadows made him think more of music than hills and valleys. It brought to mind a piece of classical music he had once heard that was supposed to have been inspired by the natural world. Something his wife listened to. What he was seeing was in such contrast to what he was hearing from Berry, that he wondered why his mind had gone there.

He realized Berry had asked a question, and he had missed it.

"Redd, you still with me?"

"Oh yes, sorry, I am just processing all of this. What did you ask?"

"I just asked if you were clear on all of this so far."

"Oh sure, way too clear. Go ahead. Tell me the rest."

"This is where it gets nastiest. The crew on the chopper was up for going after the locals and Ashby apparently lost it. The report didn't say if he had his own weapon or not. And I don't think that he, even as a private security person, should have been allowed to participate in any sort of raid. I would think not. You know about some of the cases with the private guys in Iraq, so I am thinking not.

"But be that as it may, the chopper crew leaves two people to secure the site, again probably not kosher, and lifts off with Ashby and some gunners. They come up on a group of people, but it's not clear if this is the same group that was at the plane. Never will know now. They set the chopper down and Ashby and a couple of guys jump out. Intentions aren't clear. The report later says the pilot saw that there were women and children in the small group, and they were probably non-combatants. But Ashby headed for them, and before he could be stopped, he had killed a woman carrying a baby. In fact, he shot through the baby and blew out the woman's chest. He then shot a boy, maybe twelve or so, shot another young man, and was aiming on another woman when the soldiers subdued him. This was all pretty close up and pretty fast and intense, but Ashby was apparently wearing one of those head camera things, a GoPro? And recorded some of it.

"I don't know if you were ever in a situation like that or not. I assume not. But things can get out of hand quickly. I don't have the follow up, but it seems they got Ashby back on the chopper, went back and picked up the other two soldiers and the bodies and went back to the base. From what I know, an investigation was launched into this along about the time of the last election. The incident itself is over five years old. But if you recall the recent pardon after the court martial of an officer? The environment for punishing this sort of thing isn't getting much support, especially when it's a brave civilian protecting our country from the Arab hordes."

Herring had forgotten the music on the mountains and was paying full attention at this point. "I am both surprised and sickened and yet not surprised at all," he said. "When you think that the US has a military presence in a hundred countries on the planet, I guess in some ways I am surprised things like this don't happen more often."

"That aside," replied Berry, "I think you can see how what happened up by Turkey has direct relevance to the first three coffins, and why it seems like we have the link we were looking for. And if Ashby did have footage of the massacre and was able to hold onto it, it appears that whoever did this must have gotten hold of it and used it to stage the warnings."

"But what was the purpose of a warning?" asked Herring.

"I don't know unless it was to terrorize him a bit before killing him, or maybe threaten to use the photos unless he paid out some money to the group? Probably too much of a stretch to think it might have been money for the victims. Or it could maybe have been someone else who got hold of the photos and was looking to blackmail him. The soldiers on the chopper? We need to look at them. But I don't see that."

"But where would the pictures have been? This isn't something you show anybody, I wouldn't think. These are war crimes."

"That's why we need to find that laptop. I'm guessing they were stored there, probably encrypted and hidden in a password protected file no one could easily access."

Herring was not sure how to take all of this information.

"Wendell, in some ways what you told me moves things along, but in others it just adds more confusing layers and obstacles. We have what might be a motive, but no link to a probable perpetrator, and nothing else. No link to the means, no idea how the opportunity arose or was capitalized on, and no laptop to learn anything from. I think I'm happy you're taking it over.

"Given what you seem to know and what you've told me, I think I agree that Kathryn is not a target at this point. It would prove nothing, and they would have killed her to punish Ashby, if anything."

"Yes, that's my conclusion," agreed Berry. "I don't think it would hurt for you to keep an eye on things for a bit. Pretty easy on the eyes anyway. I'll let the state know to pull their patrols."

"Okay," replied Herring. "I'll run out there and tell her we're pulling the troopers. I assume we don't discuss any of what you just told me?"

"Oh Lord no. I think you should just tell her the FBI and other agencies are investigating, and that it appears to have strong connections to the plane and spy business, and we'll let her know if we arrest someone. Pretty lame, I know, but that's as far as we can go."

Lame was right, but Herring didn't have a better idea. He thanked Berry and hung up. By now it was noon. This time when he stopped at Mike's on his way to the farm, he decided to take a chance and pick up the one vegetarian option for Kathryn. A mushroom and corn quesadilla to go with his own BLT.

19

Hidden Feelings

When Herring arrived at Kathryn's house, the trooper was just getting the message that he was no longer needed. He was headed to the door to tell Kathryn, whose pickup was in the driveway.

Herring thanked him for being there and told him he would tell Kathryn. He went through the back gate and knocked. Kathryn appeared from the front of the house and motioned for him to enter. She was once again wearing tight work jeans and a plaid shirt and a down vest. It seemed to be a kind of uniform. Herring had been trying his best to keep a professional distance mentally. And to keep his thoughts on something other than her fit and well-proportioned body and her lovely, if slightly stern, face. Now that they had concluded that she was neither a suspect nor likely to be in danger, the attraction he had barely managed to suppress was rising to the surface.

He had not been interested in another relationship after his wife died. At least not for the first year. After that, a couple of well-meaning friends had tried to set him up with several women close to his age, but he had felt awkward. The set-up dates had not been intellectually interesting enough to pursue beyond a first night out for a meal. His position as sheriff also seemed to be a hindrance to conversation. One or two of his dates had wanted to pry for inside information, and one had wanted to know how he could stand to do his job. He finally rejected any further attempts to set him up.

"I hope you don't mind," he said to Kathryn, "but I was picking up something for lunch, and this time I thought I would bring something along for you. I took a chance on it being vegetarian?"

Kathryn smiled at him and motioned him to sit at the table near the doors. "That was very nice of you. I haven't had lunch yet today and vegetarian is fine. I'm not a die-hard vegetarian, but it's easier in lots of ways. Forget that for now. What do you have to report?"

Herring filled her in on what he and Berry had agreed to, that it appeared the attack was based on something related to her father's work. And investigations were continuing from a military and security standpoint. He didn't say terrorist since he didn't want to alarm her. He did say that the FBI might want to talk to her at some point, but that was out of his realm of control. He told her it might be a week before the bodies were released. She had, surprisingly, not heard from Caroline's family and had not tried to call them. Herring tucked this bit of info away for future thought. All families are dysfunctional, some are just more dysfunctional than others.

After catching Kathryn up, Herring's attention went back to eating lunch.

"You mentioned earlier that vegetarian was easier. How is that? It seems to be it's harder to get all you need from vegetables."

"Oh, just simple things. You can make a vegetable stew and leave it on the stove in a cool kitchen for days on end, and it'll be fine. If you had meat in it, you'd have to refrigerate and divide and store and so on. And it's not hard to get what you need from vegetables if you include some protein from beans and dairy."

"I guess that makes sense. I can cook the basics but eating alone doesn't inspire me to branch out or think about new ways to do things. Eating alone isn't much fun, so you don't put much effort into what's on the table. I guess you know that better than me." He smiled, but also flushed a little. "I probably shouldn't have said that. You seem to be better at it than I am."

Kathryn smiled back. "No offense taken. I guess I never wanted to admit it, but I must have a few of the same characteristics as Douglas. We are brother and sister after all. It's probably what makes me good with genetics, the attention to detail, the singular focus. The ability or desire to be left alone."

"Not sure I understand. You adjust to what you are given, or you will go a little crazy. It took my wife and me a while to accept that we could not have children. But eventually it sunk in, and we got on with our lives. Her outlet, or whatever you would call it, was through teaching. She really cared for her students, really felt love for many of them, and wanted to direct them as she would have directed kids of ours."

"I'm sorry for that. It must have been very difficult. For me, I think I fell into a kind of tomboy thing growing up and skipped a lot of girlie wishes. We were army brats for a time, which toughens you up. And boys hate girls with brains. And if you aren't amazed by all the things boys have to offer, you must be a lesbian. So, I let them think that."

This was a slightly more direct conversation about gender roles than Herring was used to. Kathryn smiled at him across the table. "Am I making you uncomfortable, Redd?"

Herring flushed and looked away. "Yes and no."

"You mean you are, but you don't want to be."

"That's probably right. I don't want to say the wrong thing."

"Well, let me help. If I *am* a lesbian, you are off the hook emotionally. Then you just have to decide whether I am interesting enough to be a friend. But if I'm not a lesbian, then you have to figure out what's wrong with me, and whether it's too dangerous to let your thoughts roam where they might. You may not know this, but women almost immediately know when a man is interested in them. And at what level. Since I am not a normal woman in most people's eyes, it might surprise you that I know this."

Redd was now wishing he had simply called her and told her she didn't need the trooper around anymore. He thought he had kept his feelings deeply hidden. In reality he had been attracted to her from the moment he met her. He had admired her poise the first night. Had respected her care and concern for her cattle. Had found her physically attractive at all levels. Was intrigued by the psychological links to her brother and her understanding of him, and her willingness to facilitate his dream of isolation.

"I apologize. I didn't think I was so obvious. I honestly don't know…"

"You don't need to apologize," she replied with emphasis on apologize. "I like your company. I actually like the age difference. You just need to think about it. I have stuff to do at the farm now. Thanks for the lunch." With that she cleared away the paper wrappings from the lunch and gave him a light kiss on the cheek. "Bye."

20

Paperwork

Herring drove back to the office. He realized he had let everything he normally said grace over be taken care of by Roddie and Blaine. And they had done so with no complaints. Blaine was once again out on a domestic abuse call at the edge of Staunton, the kind of call that all of the officers hated to face. Roddie gave Herring a list of calls that had come in over the past three days. Half of them involved assault, and a third had something to do with a vehicle. Some involved both assault and a vehicle, as in the hit-and-run. More like a bump-and-run, when an irate husband had tried to run down his wife's boyfriend, but got his pickup stuck in a ditch before he could do much damage. The boyfriend turned out to have missed a court date. And the wife was in possession of heroin, so now all three were in the cells awaiting a bail hearing. Fortunately, not the same cell.

Herring also perused the national database to see if anything caught his eye relative to the coffins or the murders, but nothing jumped out. This database is called the National Crime Information Center or NCIC and contains seven stolen property categories, and ten person categories, one of which is Violent

Gang & Terrorist Organization. He found nothing local or regional that would fit the case. On the local level, there were the usual notices and warnings. Two wanted notices from the surrounding counties, one for burglary and one for wounding a law officer and escaping custody. Most of the rest were failures to appear in court, or parole violations. So someone would need to try to find those people now, taking up valuable time and resources.

In addition to the serious items, Herring also quickly glanced at a site that featured stupid crimes around the nation. Key West was frequently highlighted. He found a video of a man jumping off the dock onto a pelican, for which he received a ninety-day sentence. And another individual who had pulled a gun on someone who accused him of having a small penis because he kept revving his Jeep engine and annoying a group of people.

Herring logged off of the search sites and onto the county reporting site to write and file the required reports on his activities, vehicle use, and the like. Reporting and paperwork, more properly computer work, took up an increasing percentage of his and his deputies' time. He wondered if some day that would be all they would get done.

By four o'clock he had completed his reports. He needed to stop by the grocery store and restock some essentials and figure out something for dinner for the next few days. He wanted to make a contribution to the Thanksgiving dinner at Roddie's but couldn't decide what to take. There would already be too much food so maybe a bouquet of flowers from the produce department.

Thinking back over the past few days, he'd had very little desire to go home and grill a steak on the gas grill and bake a potato and eat alone. But he also wasn't confident enough to call Kathryn and ask her if she would like to go out to dinner. He was certainly nowhere near asking her to come to his place.

He stepped over to Blaine's desk and looked at the word-of-the-day. It was *satisfice, to choose or adopt the first satisfactory option that one comes across.* At one level he thought it had a bit of relevance to his current situation but didn't come close to capturing the strength of his real feelings.

21

November

Herring had not called Kathryn the evening before, as much as he had wanted to. After stopping by the grocery, he had gone home and grilled the steak and baked a potato after all. But the steak was flavorless and the potato had hard spots, and the plastic box of mixed greens he thought he should use up had a lot of wilted leaves. After dousing it with some store-bought vinaigrette and taking two bites, he threw it out.

It had been dark when he got home, so no time for an evening walk up the hill behind his house. He had seen a pair of foxes a week or so earlier and he hoped they were still in the area. They had been playing at the edge of the woods in a small grassy area and had stared at him for a long time before retreating behind the cover of the trees. There were reports of bears along the ridges in the western part of the county where the hills were steeper and mostly still covered with woods. The eastern half of the county was flatter until you got to South River, and more of the land was dedicated to crops.

A hundred years earlier there had been more woodland. Most farmers kept a patch of old-growth trees, and when they needed lumber, they would hire a forester and a lumberman to cull mature oaks, and maybe some pines. They'd haul the logs to the sawmill and have them cut into fence boards and joists and siding for the barn and house repairs. Now, most barns are metal, and the woodlands are often poorly maintained. He had read somewhere that there were 331 species of trees and shrubs in the forests of the Blue Ridge mountains in Virginia, but that number seemed low to Herring.

He had not slept well Wednesday night. On Thursday morning, he called Berry and asked if he had an update, but Berry had nothing that would move anything along. It was now five days since the discovery of the bodies. For the most part nothing much more was known now than had been known at the time of discovery. And it was Thanksgiving, so nothing would happen today. Berry told him they would most likely release the bodies for burial or cremation by the following Monday. Herring would relay this message to Kathryn, who would need to go back to Monterey to tell Douglas.

He had no idea how Kathryn and Douglas would work this out with Caroline's family. He also wondered if anyone had been in touch with the family attorney relative to the will or trust. Kathryn had not seemed to think it would alter much of her life, and Douglas didn't care. Herring assumed it wouldn't make much difference to Caroline's family either, but it still needed to be addressed pretty quickly for all sorts of legal reasons. He had almost forgotten about the ownership in the aircraft business and wondered why no one from that company had been in touch. Or maybe they had, and Kathryn had not considered it his business. Needing to tell Kathryn about the release of the bodies gave him an excuse to go back to the farm.

Herring couldn't say he was looking forward to dinner with Roddie and Barb and their whole extended family. There are places he would rather be. But they had invited him every year since Mary died, and he appreciated it. And it was probably good for him to be in the company of some folks who had something to talk about other than coffins. Barb outdid herself with the feast, and he went home full and fell asleep watching TV.

Kathryn's pickup was not at the house when he arrived the next morning, so he headed to the barns where they had gone to inspect the heifers. She wasn't there either. He drove back out by the landing strip and went up the hill and turned into the main house driveway. He saw her pickup parked near the garage, in the same area as the evening of the meeting with the FBI.

He pulled up next to it and went to the back doorway of the house. The door was open except for a screen. The temperature was only in the high fifties, but the sun on the back walkway made it feel much warmer. He knocked on the screen door but got no response. He opened the screen door, stepped inside and called her name.

He heard a chair move, and she appeared in a doorway halfway down a short hallway on the left.

"Well, hello, Redd, I'm glad to see you. I have a lot of interesting news. Come on in."

"I can't say that I have news, so I'm happy to hear that you do. How are you doing?"

"I'm fine. Busy. Half of our heifers have eaten down their grass, so I had to start them on protein cubes and some hay this morning. Another year or two and I'm going to figure out how to have grass year-round."

"I'm glad to hear you're able to focus on the job at hand. So what news do you have?"

"The first thing is a registered letter from a law firm in Richmond. They appear to represent Caroline's parents. I was up here when the postman came today, and he had a couple of interesting items that required signatures, but this is the most interesting. The letter is to me, but sent here to the farm, so I guess they don't know I live down the hill. And it states

that when the bodies are released, they want sole control of
Caroline's remains for a private funeral service. It also states
that they explicitly do *not* want to have Ashby's body released
to them. And they do not want to participate in his service, and
they do not want me to attend Caroline's service or communicate with them, other than through this law firm. It feels like
they think *I* killed her or something.

"And I got a letter from the estate attorneys expressing
condolences, saying there was no rush for me to contact them.
And then another letter dictated the same day, asking that I get
in touch as soon as possible. Both were registered. And both
were to be delivered to my house, but the postman had me sign
for them up here. I don't know why the attorneys couldn't just
call. I was about to call them when you drove up."

"Anything else?"

"Just one thing. I had a call from an attorney from the
aviation company wanting to know when they could come
and get the airplane. Father apparently didn't own it but had
it on some kind of lease. I told them the FBI would have to
release it first. They towed it into the hangar and have it locked
and sealed up."

"That's a pretty full plate for one morning. Do you want
me to wait outside while you call the estate guy?"

"No, just wait here. I'll call him now." Herring was seated
at the side of the desk, and as Kathryn said this, she reached
over and squeezed his arm gently and smiled.

She dialed using the desk phone, a rarity anymore. And
after punching the keys a few times for English versus Spanish
and putting in the extension, she was connected to a live person.

"Hi, this is Kathryn Ashby. I am calling about the two letters
your firm sent. I don't think I've met you. I think we worked
with someone named Wagner when a lot of these documents
were drawn up. So, what's up?"

Herring could hear a voice coming through the earpiece but couldn't make out any words. There was what must have been more condolences as Kathryn replied with thanks, and yes, she was surprised too, and so on.

Then the conversation shifted. Kathryn was taking notes on a lined legal pad and frowning. "I'm sorry, would you repeat that?" She was sitting upright stiffly and holding the pen above the paper. "When was this done?" Another pause.

"But never signed."

"He was planning to take the land out of the trust?"

"Wouldn't he have had to talk to me first?"

"You're kidding."

"When was he planning to sign all of this?"

"When? After Europe?"

"So as of now, nothing has changed?"

Herring could hardly stand it. He could imagine what was being said on the other end of the line. Kathryn was now visibly shaking. She said into the phone, "I need to process this. I'll call you back."

She hung up and looked at Herring with tears in her eyes. She stood up and he did also. She walked over to him and looked into his eyes and said softly, "Would you just hold me for a moment?" And started to cry.

After a few minutes, her shaking stopped, and she pushed away and wiped at the tears in her eyes. She found a tissue and blew her nose. "Let's go out in the living room and let me tell you what almost happened. I'm glad you're here because otherwise I think I might have been your prime suspect."

She took him by the hand and led him out to the living room. They sat down side by side on the sofa that was positioned to look out onto the pastures below. The barns and the runway and hundreds of black cattle dotted the landscape. Kathryn held onto his hand and studied the view.

"You know, money and things aren't all that important to me. I was never going to own this land, just use it and raise these cattle and do something in the end that I think is beneficial. And I never considered that it might be threatened. You know, the prenup, the generation skipping trust, all of that."

She paused. Herring remained silent. "So, what the attorney just told me was that I was on the verge of having that all taken away. Not tomorrow, but soon most likely."

"How?" said Herring. "I thought prenups were permanent, and I didn't think taking apart trusts was that easy."

"Well, it turns out, prenups can be altered any time as long as both parties agree to the changes. And my father was going to sign a new one along with altering the trust to take the land out so that Caroline would have greater shared control. We didn't talk about the cattle, so I don't know what he had in mind there. I can't believe it, my own father. I mean, we weren't all that close anymore, but we were civil. I know Caroline hated me and he knew it too, but he couldn't have run the cattle business without me, and didn't even get that excited about it anymore. But to do this…" she trailed off.

"You said almost. So I take it, nothing got signed?"

"According to the attorney, the new prenup was ready for signing but the transfer out of the trust was more complicated and there were tax specialists looking at it. Apparently Caroline's family's tax people, not ours. That's why I never heard anything. I don't know enough tax law to know if there would have been implications or not. I do know I was not a signatory because I was the generation being skipped for inheritance purposes."

"But as a result of their deaths," Herring paused, "nothing has changed?"

"Exactly. So there would be a pretty good motive, wouldn't there? Thank God I was camping."

"But you didn't know about it."

"As far as I know, nobody but Caroline and my father and the attorneys knew about it. So I guess the motive disappears after all."

"Your father hadn't hinted at it? Acted strange?"

"No, I hadn't seen much of him lately. We don't have any sales coming up. He and Caroline have a place at Hilton Head, and they were there for much of the fall. None of this showed up on our business computer or in any emails. I guess he had it on his laptop that is now missing."

"If this had gone through, what would it have done to you?"

"That's just it, I don't know. Maybe nothing immediately, but if he was taking the land here out of the trust and giving Caroline control, then if anything happened to him, she could then sell the land and I would have nowhere to go with all of the cattle. I'm half owner of those, but this land is worth ten or fifteen million dollars, and I'm a little short of the cash to replace it if I had to."

"Is the attorney going to send you copies of the proposed changes?"

"I don't know, I was so shocked I didn't ask. I'm sorry I broke down. This is such a horrible betrayal. I just don't get it. We were never *that* much at odds, I didn't think. I don't know, maybe I didn't really know my father at all. And with all this FBI stuff and Middle East connections, I guess I really have been in the dark. And you don't have anything to enlighten me with on that front either?"

Herring thought about it for a minute. She had just received a huge blow, and while the outcome looked favorable, this was coming on top of the murders and a complicated back story, and no identifiable culprits. He would not add to the mix with details from Berry's findings. "There may or may not be anything from the FBI. I don't have anything I can tell you about that yet."

"Can't tell me or won't tell me?"

"I can't tell you, but even if I could, it wouldn't shed any light on the murders. There isn't a single shred of evidence pointing to anyone or any group."

"But the FBI and all those other people are looking at it anyway. So they think the roots are there?"

She was not to be distracted. Not from the core mystery of a pair of killings that were highly ritualistic, not from her father's work on the clandestine side of the military, not from the disappearance of most of the materials and computers that could shed light on some of it. She was accustomed to thinking in complicated patterns as a geneticist. In some ways this was an analogy for a genetic string that needed decoding. Put all the pieces into the machine and after a while it would spit out an answer. It occurred to Herring that if he could give all the pieces to Douglas, Douglas could probably determine enough of the probabilities to guide them in the right direction. But that was never going to happen.

Herring decided to deflect from the discussion with more immediate items. "What do you want to do now? Get the proposed changes from the attorneys? Just thinking about it, and based on some cases we have been involved in at the county level, I would recommend you get another independent attorney of some repute involved, to insure you can't be sued by Caroline's family. I don't see how they could, but wills and trusts can turn out to be some of the most highly litigious documents in the world. She didn't have kids, or none we know of, so that should make it simpler, but I wouldn't take anything for granted. You know how this country is. Everybody sues everybody."

"Yeah, I don't even know if Caroline's parents knew about any of this. I really don't know them at all. There is certainly some bitterness there, so maybe they did know and had hoped to share in the wealth, and now their hopes are dashed. Caroline has a brother who works with her father, I think. I met him once or twice up at the house. I didn't care for him. Too much like his mother and too old-time southern. I guess none of them want me around. The letter from their attorney certainly made that clear."

Kathryn rubbed her hand over her face and sighed. "I have a bunch of work to do. I'll make a list. I have heifers to move this afternoon."

"If I could ride a horse, I'd offer to come and help."

Kathryn grinned at him. "Don't you have a job, arresting people and giving out tickets and stuff?"

Herring blushed again. "Oh, I have some flexibility in responsibilities. We're in the pre-Christmas lull right now. Actually, I really should get back to the office. I forgot we have a budget prep meeting coming up. We're behind on that, and there's no money for most of the things we need anyway, so we haven't been taking it as seriously as we should."

They were still sitting side by side. Herring was reluctant to stand up. He liked the warmth of her body next to his and her profile was just as lovely as the sight of her straight on. If he had been in high school, he probably would have tried to kiss a girl he was seated that close to. But the atmosphere and all of the disturbing news made it seem like that would be an exploitation of emotions. He frowned and stood, and she stood also.

"You know, I will have to tell my FBI friend, Wendell, about this. I don't think it fits with where they are headed, but you never know. I suppose there could be some element of black-mail. I have to think it through. I hate the invasion of privacy, but I probably need copies of some of the letters."

"Redd, I really do need to deal with the heifers right now. Why don't you find out what you need to take to your friend and come back this evening? I have some split pea soup with ham. You stop by that new bakery in town and bring some of their bread and dessert, and we can go over what you need and copy it."

Herring turned and gave her a hug. He was amazed at how much joy he felt at that instant. He leaned to give her a kiss on the cheek, but she turned her head and kissed him lightly on the lips and smiled and said, "See you at six."

Herring drove back to the office feeling lighter in spirit than he had felt for a long time. He was well aware of the saying "there's no fool like an old fool." He sincerely hoped he wasn't setting himself up for such a role. On the other hand, she was the one who had been making the overtures. And she wasn't a gold digger since he had no gold to dig. She was the one with the gold, and everything else. He really hoped he wouldn't screw it up.

By the time he got to the office he had pulled himself together and was focused on what he had learned. He was beginning to formulate some new questions about the past seven or so weeks. He called Wendell and briefly reported Kathryn's shocking news.

"That's an interesting set of developments," said Berry, after listening to Herring describe the changes to the two documents and the contents of the letter about the funeral. "It certainly throws a new light on it and provides a motive."

"Wendell, I've been thinking about this since she told me. I don't think we can make many inferences on anything until we get the documents from the attorneys and establish a timeline. Think about it, the first coffin was out there six weeks before the killings. Now unless the coffin was totally unrelated to the trust and prenup changes, which I find hard to believe, there must have been some sort of blackmail thing going on."

"How do you mean?"

"Okay, the coffins had to be a warning. We have to establish that Ashby actually saw the coffins or a picture or something. By the way, where are you on that?"

"Oh, I meant to tell you, they gave it to one of the women who specializes in document reconstruction, but she has been out with the flu. She should be back tomorrow. I'll see if we can get that moved along."

"Alright, let's propose this scenario: Someone learns about Ashby's evil deeds in Iraq and gets copies of some photos from somewhere, and calls him up and asks for money to not put them out there. Or emails him or whatever. Sends a note. Now, if you or I got a warning in the mail or by phone or however, what would we do?"

"Since I don't have any deeds that bad in my past, I would think it was a hoax."

"So would I," said Herring, "and so might Ashby, even knowing what he had done. How can you prove the photos are ones he took? Supposedly he isn't in any of them holding up a head or some such gruesome thing. Plus you can photoshop anything these days. Even I know that."

"I think I'm beginning to get where you are going."

"Right, so he ignores the call or letter, and the blackmailer now decides to send a stronger message. He puts out another coffin with a body staged again like one of Ashby's victims in Iraq. Still, though, we have to figure out how he let Ashby know. I guess we assume a picture sent and we need to find it. At the same time, Ashby is supposedly rewriting his trust agreement and his prenup. Why was he doing that? Was he trying to transfer his money to his wife so that the blackmailers couldn't get to it? That seems pretty naive at first glance. But maybe he still wasn't taking the blackmailer seriously and was just shielding, not thinking he might be in mortal danger.

"My response, I think, would be to assume that the

worst-case scenario would be great embarrassment, and maybe a divorce if the Iraq stuff came out. Because if someone kills me, they get nothing. I don't think he would have been afraid of getting killed. Besides, he was a macho, somewhat violent guy at times and probably figured he could protect himself."

"You're spinning a pretty fancy and complicated tale there, Redd."

"I am just trying to come up with some scenarios that make sense. If what I just said makes any sense, then it has to follow that the blackmailer, turned killer, kept threatening with more coffins with examples of the bodies back in Iraq, Ashby kept resisting but continued to work on asset shifting, thinking he had plenty of time. And suddenly one day the killer shows up, having either given up on the money, or coming to demand it in person, and ends up killing them both. The more I think about it, the more I think the killer just screwed up all the way around. I don't think he had credibility with Ashby, so Ashby slow played him, or her. I think maybe he decided to confront Ashby in person and panicked and maybe killed him by mistake and then had to kill Caroline as well. He was smart enough to take the cell phones and the computer and lucked out there in getting most of the evidence. I don't think a home-grown terrorist did this. But it was somebody who knew what Ashby had done. So that opens up a whole roomful of potential, and most of them would be people you would have to identify and research. I would guess."

"Redd, you ought to just stick to cattle rustling or whatever it is you all do down there in the valley. I'm not saying you are wrong, but this is a completely different tack. I do think we need a timeline for the prenup and trust work as you said. I think since this is a murder, we don't have any attorney client privilege. Kathryn Ashby seemingly isn't a suspect. Can you start gathering those documents? And I will see about getting the photo lady back on reconstruction of the pictures. Let's build a timeline from beginning to end. Let's talk tomorrow."

Herring hung up feeling frustrated, but also feeling like talking it through had begun the process of opening up a path to finding the killer.

It was still early afternoon, so Herring decided to create a template that he could later fill in with details from the attorneys.

1. Date of the first verbal warning or request? Was there one, or did the killer just start with the first coffin? What was the date of the first meeting by Ashby with estate and prenup attorneys?

Oct 8 First coffin discovered

2. Was there any response to killer? Any meetings with attorneys following this event?

Oct 22 Second coffin discovered

3. Same as above. Any new meetings with attorney? Where was Ashby all this time? Ashby and Caroline had been in Hilton Head for a lot of the autumn. Check out Ashby's schedule and use of the airplane or commercial flights. There were no nonstops or even reasonable connections from the Shenandoah Valley to Hilton Head, so Ashby would have used his own plane for any travel. A detail for one of the deputies to check out. Where and how?

Nov 6 Third, most troublesome coffin

It now occurred to Herring that by this point, Ashby should have connected the figures in the coffins with the people he had killed in northern Iraq. The coffin with the baby and the mother should have certainly triggered the strongest memory. He was only guessing about the events of the first month or so. If Ashby had not tied the images in the first two coffins to Iraq, then maybe he only began to take the warning seriously a few weeks before his death.

And maybe he still never took it completely seriously. But for some reason he did fly back over to the farm the day of his death, when he should have been headed for Dulles airport and Europe. Too many moving pieces and too little information. He needed the dates and materials from the attorneys. And Ashby's laptop and phone would make all the difference.

22

Split Pea Soup

Herring finished his notes and a list of administrative duties around five. He left the SUV in the parking lot, even though by rights he could, and maybe should, have driven it home in case he was called out during the night. He had a portable radio that connected to the dispatcher, so if need be, he could swing by and pick up his official vehicle. He wasn't sure of all of the impulses behind the decision to drive his old pickup truck, but he knew what a few of them were.

At the bakery he picked out a couple of fruit tarts with glazed strawberries, blueberries, and mandarin orange slices on top, a couple of crème caramels, and just for good measure, two almond croissants to leave with Kathryn for breakfast. Also a nice baguette. He had only been to the bakery once or twice before, but the smell of the French bread and the appearance of the croissants made his mouth water and he promised himself that he'd come back soon. He recalled his trips to France with his wife, and how well they had eaten. She would always vow to cook more like the French when they got home. But the pressure of everyday life and the lack of the same ingredients soon put those vows to rest, and they were back to the normal American meals.

The gate to Kathryn's patio was open and there were lights around the flower beds even though the flower season was long gone. He could see her setting out bowls and silverware through the glass doors. She had changed from the tight work jeans and plaid shirt that seemed to be her daily uniform into a pair of black, almost silky looking slacks. While not as tight as her normal jeans, the slacks fit snugly and accentuated the length and shape of her legs. They stopped just above her ankles, which even at that distance he could see were thin. He had always been attracted to thin ankles. Her top was a long-sleeved silk blouse in blue-gray that buttoned up the front and had a collar like a dress shirt. The buttons were little white pearls, and he assumed they went all the way to the top, but at the moment the top two were open showing just a hint of cleavage. The sleeves had French cuffs which were pushed up almost to her elbows. She was barefoot and her hair was pulled back into a French bun, accentuating the shape of her face. She looked like she should be in Paris instead of on a farm in Virginia.

He took all this in while walking across the patio to the doors. And then he stopped dead in his tracks. What a moron I am, what a hick, what an idiot, he thought. It never occurred to him to go home and change out of this uniform. The phrase "beauty and the beast" popped into mind. At this point Kathryn saw him standing there and came to the door and opened it. "What are you doing out there? Come on in."

"I'm, sorry, I wasn't thinking. I should have gone home and put on something more casual."

"Oh stop. I had to change, one of the heifers pooped on me." She grinned.

"Yeah, I see, well you look lovely. I'll at least take off the holster and tie."

"Just put them on the table over there. The soup is reheating." She took the bags with the pastries and the bread. "I have some stuff for you to look at. I called the attorneys who were working on my father's estate plan and the prenup. They emailed me drafts of the whole mess. I printed it and we can look at it after we eat."

"Amazing, that was fast. No questions asked?"

"No, I think they feel a little embarrassed. They were involved in this little coup behind my back and now I'm in charge and they'll have to deal with me. They're trying to be nice. I'm sure this is lucrative. Or was."

"How long has this been in the works? Or can you tell?"

"Oh yes, longer than I thought. Sometime in mid-September at the latest. They sent a copy of an email from him to them. He asked for them to look into prenup changes, not specified at that point, and also the implications of pulling a significant portion of the assets out of the trust. There is some later stuff on options, but this had been going on for a while."

"Well, Kathryn, I don't know that it means much, but I am really sorry this was going on behind your back. I don't know much of anything about your relations or work with your father, but this is really awful. Is there any indication of what was driving the decision? This is before any of the warnings that we know about popped up. Does he mention any of that in the email?"

"No, not in that one, but I haven't looked at everything. We can look at it after we eat. Would you slice a bit of the baguette and pop it in the toaster? We'll have that and some blue cheese and a little salad with the soup."

Herring took the bread out of the wrapper and sliced a half dozen slices on a cutting board that was already out on the table next to a high-end four-slice toaster. When he pushed the little lever down that lowered the bread, it stayed down and felt snug, unlike the cheap toaster that he used at home. His popped up four times before staying down, and then burned the bread no matter what the setting. Everything in the house and kitchen was of high quality. The bread knife had some Japanese characters on it and the blade was deep and looked like it was made of pounded layers. It seemed too important to just slice bread. It was exceptionally sharp. There was real silverware on the table, and cloth napkins with a blue edge. The table itself was a lighter pine in color and the chairs were matching and sturdy but comfortable. Everything had that designer feel, but it was too comfortable with too many personal touches for it to have been purely a designer's effort. Herring decided that since he couldn't even remember to dress appropriately for a dinner he was looking forward to, he probably shouldn't attempt a conversation about the room and its features. He might make an even greater fool of himself.

"I don't know if you drink wine or not, but a little Pinot Noir would go nicely with this."

"Oh yeah, I have that every night," laughed Herring. "Sure, I'm up for trying it. I don't know one wine from another, but if you know how to pronounce that, I'm guessing you do."

"I actually do know a little bit about wine. I don't drink it every day, but in spite of our more recent differences, my father and I used to get along, and he was way into wine. A lot of it to impress people, but still he knew his stuff, and he taught me a lot."

"Just tell me how to hold the glass and I'll try not to slurp."

Kathryn laughed. She was bringing a blue enameled pot to the table with the soup. The bread popped up from the toaster and Herring added four more slices. Kathryn put two dishes of salad on the table, already dressed with a light vinaigrette. She offered him some Bleu d'Auvergne cheese that had sat out long enough to soften and release some aroma. "Redd, you are a remarkably different man. You make me laugh. I'm wanting to make a nice meal for you and it's not scaring you, and that's just great."

"Why, was I supposed to be scared? Is this a test or something?"

"No, no, well, maybe, in a way. If I offered you a glass of wine and you said you only drank Mountain Dew at dinner, or turned up your nose at the cheese, I might have to rethink you."

"Oh, thank goodness. I'm glad I passed the test. I'd hate to get thrown out before dinner. I'm a little hungry."

They both laughed easily at that, and she motioned to one of the chairs and they sat. She ladled the soup into one of the fancy Italian-looking soup bowls that was broader and flatter than he used at home, and they began to eat, spreading a little of the bleu cheese on the bread and dipping it into the soup. The soup was a classic split pea with chunks of carrot and bits of Virginia ham that had been diced and sprinkled in after the soup had cooked with a ham hock to flavor it. The saltiness of the cheese balanced well with the soup and the Pinot Noir, a California one from the Russian Valley.

"This is wonderful," said Redd, "but I don't recall seeing that bottle of wine or that kind of cheese down at the Food Lion, not that I looked that closely. So where do you get this stuff?"

"Oh, some I order. It's amazing what you can buy online. And I stop at some of the stores in Charlottesville to stock up every now and then. The people over there around the university like to eat a little fancier than most of us here in the valley."

"Yeah, but still, you have to know what you're doing."

"Oh, are you saying a cowgirl like me can't figure this stuff out?" She paused and smiled at him. "You forget, I lived in Europe for quite a while. And yes, the food in Scotland is not exactly gourmet, but I did spend a fair amount of time in Paris. And when my mom wasn't depressed, she was a good cook."

"Yeah, I forget. Your world has been a lot different from mine in a lot of ways."

"Doesn't matter, it's how you adapt. Dessert a little later?"

"Sure, let me help clean up." He stood and helped take the dishes to the sink where Kathryn lightly rinsed them and put them into the dishwasher, silverware and all. They had not drunk much of the wine, but they left the bottle and the glasses on the table.

"Let's look at these materials for a bit. It looks like everything is a draft, but the intent is there."

She put a short stack of emails on the table. "It starts with the first email here, dated September 15. Father asked in this one, what the procedure would be for changing a prenup."

She handed the sheet to Herring, and he read it through. It was straightforward. He focused on the key concepts. "*It is my understanding that the prenuptial agreement that Caroline and I signed prior to our marriage can be changed as long as both of us are in agreement with the new terms. Am I correct in this understanding, and if so, what are the requirements, time constraints, and so forth?*"

There was no indication of why he wanted to make the changes or whether they were driven by his own desires or by a request from Caroline.

Kathryn handed him another sheet; this one has a reply from the law firm. He skipped to the relevant section. "*In short, yes you can make changes to your prenuptial agreement if both of you are in agreement as to terms. However, in your case this will not be a simple transaction for the following reasons: 1. Your prenuptial agreement includes details on disposition of property which you will need to amend or address in detail; 2. Your agreement addresses the right to sell, buy, or lease property, and you will need to amend those provisions relative to your agricultural, aircraft maintenance, and aircraft lease agreements; 3. Your prenuptial agreement specifically cites the trust or trusts that you put in place, and all of those terms will need to be addressed; 4. There are possible life insurance policies that will need to be addressed as to beneficiary; 5. There are spousal support terms that will need to be addressed; and 6. There is the area of personal rights and obligations, under which we would most likely include any contracts relative to the operation of your core business interests and any charitable or other obligations you may have in place. We will be glad to assist you in all of these areas and welcome a meeting at your earliest convenience. However, we would anticipate a timeline of three to six months depending on the details of your other agreements and obligations."*

After reading through the passage, Herring turned to Kathryn and said, "I guess I should have figured these kinds of things wouldn't be simple. But I sort of thought that in a prenup you just said, you keep what you have, and I keep what I have, in case it doesn't work out, and no hard feelings. Prenups down here are usually more like a country song where the guy keeps the pickup, the gun, and the dog, and the wife gets the kids."

Kathryn punched him but laughed. "So who gets the house?"

"The mobile home dealer—he just tows it back to town."

"That's awful, that's redneck humor."

"Hey, you forget where you live." He paused. "Just kidding. Trailer people probably aren't prenup types. But a lot of separations are sadly close to what I just said. It never works out well and the kids suffer. Anyway, what else do you have there?"

"The next set of emails seem to be lists of the items that go into all of the categories above, sort of checklists of things that would have to be worked out. I haven't taken time to look at all of it, but it is wildly complicated. And he paid out around ten thousand dollars to them at the end of September and another twenty thousand dollars in October, so they were working on a number of pieces of this. Maybe they weren't actually that far along at all. At three hundred dollars per hour that wouldn't be that much work. Hmm. I wonder if there are other people working on this, and I just don't have the information?"

"Well, I assume you will put an end to all of it now. Or just do the parts that would normally be involved if he had died a natural death. Do you have a copy of the will?"

"I know the contents, or at least I thought I did. I need to get my hands on that. I was thinking that as long as the trust hadn't changed, or the prenup, the will couldn't have either, but now I'm not so sure. God, that bastard. Or maybe that bitch of a wife. I really, really wonder what was going on here."

This last realization blindsided Kathryn. She sat looking at the papers in her hands and shaking her head. Herring stood up from his seat across from her, took the papers from her hands and looked into her eyes, moist and sad. He sympathetically pulled her to her feet and put his arms around her. She rested her head on his chest and put her arms around him and pulled him closer. After a few moments she pulled away, took him by the hand and started to lead him to the front of the house and her bedroom.

At the door she stopped and said, "I don't know how this is going to turn out with you and me, but right now I just want to have you hold me, and I want to hold you and be close to you and whatever happens, happens. Whatever it is or isn't, it's okay. You okay with that?"

Herring was as okay with that as he could possibly be. He pulled her gently toward him and kissed her on the lips. "Oh yes. Oh yes." They had forgotten dessert, there was still wine in the bottle, and the dishwasher had not been run.

23

Sleepover

Herring woke up at six o'clock to the noise of a loud truck going by outside. At first he didn't know where he was, and then things came into focus. Kathryn was not in the bed, but he heard the noise of cups and saucers being moved about in the kitchen. The night had gone so much less awkwardly than he might have foreseen. Kathryn needed to be held, and he found that for different reasons he did too. They had started tentatively, kissing, and then exploring each other's bodies. They had made love slowly and as if they were already familiar with each other, comfortable in the relationship. There was no sense of desperation or the need to rush to an ending.

They fell asleep afterward and woke again at some time in the night and made love again. Then Herring slept soundly and did not hear her get up.

He went into the bathroom, used the facilities, and washed his hands and face and squeezed a bit of toothpaste out of a tube on the sink and used his finger to rub around his teeth and gums. He found his clothes in a pile by the bed and on the back of a chair and dressed. He would have to go home and shower, shave, and change clothes before heading into the office.

In the kitchen, Kathryn came over to him, took hold of his arms, and kissed him lightly. She tasted of coffee. "Good morning. I liked last night."

Herring smiled at her. "Me too, a lot."

"You do snore a little, you know."

"Oh jeez, I'm sorry. Did I keep you awake?"

"Not long, I punched you and you stopped."

Herring felt a little embarrassed, but at the same time it felt like they had known each other forever and this was just another morning.

"Would you like coffee?" she asked. She was already dressed for a day with the cattle. She must have showered in a different bathroom because her hair looked slightly damp and he had not been awakened by bathroom noises.

"Sure, but I need to head home and change and get to the office."

"Well, I can give you a cup to go. And I see you brought two croissants for breakfast. Were you plotting to stay overnight before you got here?"

Herring blushed slightly again. He needed to get that under control. "No, not really…"

"Well, I'm not offended if you were. Did you have fun?"

Herring was not used to discussing what he had done in bed with anyone. But Kathryn was a much more direct and seemingly uninhibited person. "I had more than fun. I liked all of it."

"Well, maybe we can do that again sometime."

"That really appeals to me. But listen, we need to finish a review of your documents. What time will you finish with the cattle today? I need to call Berry and we probably need to forward some of this stuff to him, but I'd like to go over it first. I also think we need to check into Caroline's family a little more. It seems strange to me that all of a sudden your father was wanting to change all the critical estate documents after, what, ten years? What do you know about that family?"

"Not much, really, especially after I insulted her heritage. I didn't discuss her with father."

"Okay, well, let's look at it later today. What time works?"

"I should be available after two today. I have a group of cows that need to be moved and both of the guys will be there to help after we put out hay. If it suits you, I can meet you back here around then. Call me."

"That should work." Herring took the travel mug of coffee and a bag with one of the croissants and kissed her and headed out.

After showering and shaving, Herring put on a pair of jeans and button down blue and green checked flannel shirt and took a down vest off of the rack by the back door. He had adopted his own casual Friday option some time ago, but he was the only person who complied. The deputies felt like their roles demanded they appear in uniform, and they were probably right. Herring was so well-known around the town and county that it didn't much matter what he was wearing.

When he got to the office, there was a message to call Charles Austin Wilson, the chairman of the board of supervisors. He would either be perturbed that nothing was going on, or perturbed that something *was* going on. Herring would let him wait.

He scrolled through the online crime reports and found nothing new that needed immediate attention. There had been a spate of thefts overnight and both deputies were out investigating those. His department, like most, usually only recovered an average of about 15 percent of stolen items. Only a couple percent of cash or jewelry, 5 percent of office equipment and supplies, but over 50 percent of cars and trucks. Except for needing verification for insurance claims, he wondered sometimes if the victims shouldn't just file an online report with some photos of the scene and let the department put it all in their database. The computer would probably be capable of finding patterns that might lead to arrests.

When he had finished this search he called Wendell, who answered after three buzzes. "Good morning, Redd, how's progress in your area? I have a little bit to report."

"Okay, you go first."

"Our financials team pulled some details on the aircraft business up in Winchester. Ashby was only a silent partner at this point. He was more involved and invested earlier on, but not a great amount. We don't have those details. But it does appear from our sources, that Ashby's role was reduced around the time of the incident in Iraq. News must have gotten out about that, or maybe he even boasted about it, but at least within Dominion, it looks as if he became a bit of a liability. I can't give you more detail because of the security. He was kept on as a consultant, but his managerial role was reduced. He still received a fee and leased the King Air from them at a very favorable rate, so it wasn't a financial disaster for him."

"That's interesting. Is there anything in your research that shows him trying to change the flow of his income or to take out any money otherwise."

"No, not that we can tell. Why?"

"Well, he had been secretly—I say secretly because his daughter, who is his business partner at least in the cattle deal didn't know about any of it—been working to change his prenup and trusts to pull out a load of cash. I read a bunch of emails from his attorneys last night, and his prenup was so complicated it was going to take a lot of undoing. But he had started this process back in mid-September."

"Strange, that might fit the blackmail angle, but it must have been a patient blackmailer to wait that long. Or maybe he had funds he could pay out in the meantime. We need to look at that angle."

"Well, I think we need to look at his wife and her family. Ashby's daughter doesn't know much about them. They never got along, and the family never came up to the farm, or at least almost never. So if the blackmail angle is off here, the only other logical person to put pressure on him would be the wife. Especially since there is so much focus on the prenup. Interestingly, if he had done a simple prenup he could have done whatever he wanted as long as he and the wife agreed. But this one apparently was very tightly drawn and addresses almost all of the aspects of his business and personal finances. What I'm wondering is, if Caroline—who was what, fifteen years younger than he was?—maybe decided she wasn't going to be happy with an allowance, even a generous one, and figured now was the time to start making changes."

"That's all fine, but I highly doubt that it was his wife leaving coffins and wrapped up mannequins around the county to inspire him to make the changes."

"I agree, but... I know it's a long shot, but what if she had someone helping her, and the coffins were warnings to make the changes in the prenup or will or whatever, or she would ruin him with the photos, and maybe he gets prosecuted by the government?"

"Then why didn't he just divorce her and deny it all?"

"That's the question. There must be some damning evidence, and he figured divorcing her would not stop the damage. I just don't know. I don't suppose you've found any more computer records or phone records?"

"Nothing that leads anywhere. We pulled the cell phone records and his all seem to be business or legal and accounting related. And some customers for cattle. We checked. Her calls were all the regular stuff and mostly to family: mother, father, and a brother from time to time. A bunch of calls for stuff at William & Mary."

Herring thought for a moment. "I do recall Kathryn mentioning a brother. What does he do?"

"He and the father have a property development company, small time. We haven't looked very closely at it. Maybe with what you discovered about the prenup we should dig a bit."

"Well, it wouldn't hurt. None of these links make really good sense to me, but they have to tie together somehow. There is no such thing as coincidence in crime. Oh, I forgot to tell you, or maybe you got a notice from the family attorneys. They sent a registered letter to Kathryn stating that they wanted only Caroline's remains back and did not want her or her brother at any service, and they did not want Ashby's remains, or to be involved."

"Good Lord, I don't think I've ever heard of such a thing. There is some serious anger there. You would think they suspect Kathryn of killing Caroline."

"That's what Kathryn said," replied Herring. "If you think about it, maybe Caroline *was* trying to get the money for some family need, and now they are high and dry. I think you should use your infinite resources to take a look there."

"Okay, it's really not that hard. I'll get back to you. Let me know what else you find on your end. Maybe you should talk to Ashby's bankers down there. Find out from Kathryn who they deal with."

They ended the call. Herring decided he'd better get back to Wilson, so he put in a call to him.

Wilson launched right into him, "It's about damn time. I need to talk to you."

"Good morning to you, too. Sheriff Herring calling."

"Don't be a wise ass. Where are you on this case? And why are you spending so much time with the suspect?"

"I beg your pardon. We don't have a suspect; we have surviving family members. And it's the FBI's case."

"I have sources in the county, and what I hear is that you are way too deeply engaged with the relevant parties."

"I hate to disillusion you, Charles Austin, but how I conduct my part of this investigation is not open to input from the supervisors or from you. I'm assisting the FBI in trying to unravel this. This is messy."

"Yeah, well, I hear your pickup wasn't in your driveway last night and the lights were off…"

Herring felt like one of the cartoon characters with smoke coming out of its ears in rage. "Charles Austin, if I hear one more report from you on my personal movements, I will have a deputy outside your house and the house of every board member every night, making sure you are all safe from strange women and unwanted influences. Believe me." Herring knew that at least one of the board members was seeing a school-teacher who was married to someone else, and there were rumors that Wilson himself was out of town more than necessary and not always alone.

"That is an abuse of your power," said Wilson.

"Oh no, with this unsolved murder you could all be in danger. Just keeping you safe." With that Herring hung up. He had said more than he should, and at base he knew that his relationship with Kathryn was definitely not appropriate while the investigation was going on. He had known that almost from the minute he met her, and he had also known on some level, that he was willing to put his job at risk.

Over the past couple of days, he had begun to realize how lonely he had been. In spite of his ability to campaign for the job of sheriff, and his ability to meet with and talk to groups of people with confidence, he was essentially a solitary person. His grandfather, who was an old-time, self-taught country lawyer, had been a great reader and had given Herring books over the years. For a long time, Herring didn't pay much attention to them, especially during his military years.

He was embarrassed to tell anyone, but he kept a copy of Marcus Aurelius' *Meditations* on his bedside table and most nights would thumb through and read a few of the paragraphs. He had been surprised from the beginning how pertinent and universal so many of the thoughts were. Especially for a Roman emperor who was in power for nineteen years. He had thought of the emperors as ruthless, scheming autocrats whose most frequent thoughts must have been about how to stay in power. He had read somewhere that a number of statesmen and world leaders over the years had also referred frequently to the *Meditations*. The sentiments expressed there ranged from personal advice that a columnist in an American paper might give, to passages that could have come from the New Testament.

Herring had not found many references to grief when his wife died. Supposedly Aurelius' wife—his cousin and the daughter of the former emperor—had been wildly unfaithful, but Aurelius had either not known or not cared.

Now, Herring felt that his own course, relative to both the investigation and to his relationship with Kathryn, would fit one of Aurelius' maxims to be true to your instincts and yourself.

24

Turks and Caicos

Herring left the office at noon and stopped at a local sandwich shop just up the road for something to eat. Just as he was finishing, the cell phone that Wendell had given him vibrated in his pocket. He told Wendell to hold on a minute, put his tray back on the serving counter and stepped outside.

"That was quick, what's up?"

"Two things, and I have no idea where they fit. Actually, three things. First, you remember I told you there was a little growth on Ashby's brain?"

"Yes, vaguely."

"Well, we just got back an analysis, and it would not have been apparent yet, and we don't know if Ashby was even aware of it, but the pathologist is pretty certain it would shortly have developed into an inoperable tumor."

"So, we need some medical records. That's quite interesting."

"Yes, but he might not have known about it."

"What next?"

"This is even more interesting. It turns out that Caroline's father and her brother were in some serious financial difficulties. It looks like they made a plunge into a hotel and condo venture in the Turks and Caicos and got hit by that last hurricane just as they were getting close to completion. The insurance company is refusing to honor the claim saying they didn't properly secure the premises from rain and wind damage. I'm surprised Ashby never mentioned this to Kathryn."

"I don't know, maybe he did. I'll ask her. Caroline hated Kathryn for her insolence, and Kathryn didn't care for Caroline, so she says she and her father just never discussed that sort of stuff."

"Well, it's serious dollars, over ten million."

"I'm surprised it isn't more."

"It's a syndicate, so that's just their portion. Interestingly, if you cared and knew where to look, most of this information is available to the public and through filings."

"Okay, that's two things. What's the third?"

"The brother, whose name is Robert Stuart Bland Jr., is missing."

"Missing?"

"Missing, as in no one knows where he is. He was supposed to have been back in the Turks and Caicos as of Monday, and he didn't show up for a meeting."

"How do you know that?"

"I just had a call from Caroline's father, asking if we had talked to Robert. I think I told you, it took a few days to locate the parents who were out on a boat in the Bahamas. Mr. Bland had been trying to get in touch with Robert and hasn't found him."

"Oh man, that's weird. What are you going to do now?"

"Well, I just talked to Mr. Bland, so I'll alert our Miami office. They communicate with Turks, so we'll have them talk to customs in Turks and see if he ever arrived. I'm going to start a credit card search and cell phone tracking to see where he last traveled. I'll get back to you as soon as I have something. Talk to Kathryn and let me know if you learn anything."

Berry hung up. Herring stood thinking on the steps of the cafe for a moment until someone trying to get by said, "Excuse me." He apologized, stepped aside, and walked out to his vehicle and headed back to the farm.

When he arrived at Kathryn's, she was back from the morning's work and had had a light lunch.

She took his hand and gave him a brief hug as he came in. "You look like a person with things on his mind. What's up?" she said.

"Lots. Sit down, and let's go over some stuff." They sat at the table with the emails and paperwork from the prior night.

"First, do you know or did your father ever mention anything about Caroline's family's finances?"

"No, not really. He never volunteered anything, and I wasn't interested. She was kind of an off-limits subject after the vase-throwing incident."

"You didn't know that her father and her brother were in financial trouble over a development in the Turks and Caicos this fall?"

"No, I only met her brother a couple of times. At the wedding and then a couple more times up here. I didn't like him, I told you earlier. Fake Southern gentleman crap. He had an airhead date at the wedding. I do remember that. I told you, those people live in the past. But anyway, so daddy and brother have money problems? I guess that could explain father wanting to change the prenup. Caroline finally got to him. I guess I did have a reason to do the two of them in. If I had only known. And had the balls to do it."

"Don't joke. Some people don't have the same sense of humor and justice that I do. Besides, the brother, Robert, is somehow missing."

"Missing how?"

"Like missing and no one knows where he is. He was

supposed to be at a meeting on Turks and Caicos a couple of days ago, where the problem development is, and never showed up. Caroline's mom and dad just found out today."

"Well, how bad is this money problem? Maybe he just decided to split and leave his dad hanging."

"It's a big money problem from what I know, maybe ten million dollars or more."

"I still don't know how a change in the prenup would help. Or in the trust. To sell the farms to get that kind of cash? It would break up the business that made my father a lot of money. I don't see it."

Herring had been thinking about that. "I think we need to talk to your bankers and your accountants. There are ways to free up cash, but depending on what the balance sheet looks like, it might take time. And I would have thought it would have taken your permission."

"On some stuff, yes. I agree. Maybe I can get a meeting by Monday or Tuesday. Give me a minute." She left the table presumably to go find a phone number or some paperwork. He heard her talking as she leafed through some documents, in an office alcove off of the kitchen. "You up for driving to Charlottesville on Tuesday?" she yelled out to Herring.

"Sure, any time."

When she came out of the alcove she said, "That was the accountant's office. They can fill us in on Tuesday. They had been asked to look at some tax implications of different strategies but had not been told why. Nothing had been done with any of the key documents so far, to their knowledge. So that leaves the bank."

"When can we talk to them?" asked Herring.

"Not today, I'm pretty sure. Friday afternoon this late we won't catch the person we need to talk to. Monday, I'll set it up on Monday."

"Do you know if there's any debt on the farm now?"

"There's none on the cattle. Business has been very good for us. There's a couple million left on the land. I don't know the exact number. I think there was a fifteen-year mortgage for maybe eight million dollars of the purchase, maybe a little less. It should be close to being paid off. He took it out when he bought the bulk of the land and before he married Caroline. That was part of the reason for such a complicated prenup."

"I have to ask, if you don't get along, sorry, didn't get along with your father, and can't stand, sorry, couldn't stand, his wife, why did you get in this cattle business with him?"

She put her hands over her face and sighed. "At this point you might wonder." She sat and looked at the papers on the table for a bit and then at Herring. "What you have to understand is that when I agreed to get into the cattle business with father, mother had not been dead long, my father and I had actually gotten along okay for much of my life—benign neglect for much of it—but he was proud of my intelligence, and I was pretty. So that was all a good reflection on him and his genes, I guess. Unlike my poor brother, whose intelligence did him no good with my father, because he didn't have the macho, athletic, warrior, or killer instinct to go with it.

"Anyway, after I got my doctorate, I did some research in Edinburgh at the college for a couple of years, but I wanted to do something that actually produced a final product. I was already discussing teaching at several universities in the States, including UVA. Father approached me on one of his trips to Europe when I had taken the train down to London to meet him for dinner and a day in town. He had the idea of building a superior Angus herd here in the US. He would put up the money and give me a third of the profit, and third ownership in the herd, and the land would go in a trust. Plus, a free house deeded to me to live in, and full operating control. Hard to pass up when it's the literal field of your dreams. And me a pseudo-lesbian with no partner of either sex to mess up the arrangement."

At the last comment she grinned at Herring, but she could see it made him wince. "Hey, you still think that lesbian thing is real after last night?" At that they both laughed.

"So, I guess our next steps are to see what the accountants and bankers know on Monday."

"Yeah, seems like it. Did your friend Wendell tell you when they might release the bodies? I need to figure out burial or cremation plans. I need to see the will I think, to see what he wanted. I should have asked the attorneys earlier."

"Oh crap, I totally forgot. Was your father acting any different lately? Like he was sick or worried about anything?"

"No, what's this about?"

"Berry told me that during the autopsy they found the beginnings of a tumor in the brain and the pathologists best guess is that it would have evolved into an inoperable brain tumor and possibly have killed him in five years or so, after it became fully established. He never mentioned anything like that to you?"

"No, never. He wasn't very good about sickness and doctors. He would power through. He thought illness was a sign of weakness. He might not have believed it if a doctor *had* told him about it."

"Unfortunately, it's all speculative. I don't even know if that would matter. I assume they do some sort of genetic analysis or chemical analysis to make the cancer diagnosis."

"Well, I hadn't seen him much lately. I think I told you he was down in Hilton Head a lot, but when he was here, he didn't seem any different. He was off in meetings and up in Winchester a few times. Maybe he was trying to avoid me, but I just didn't notice. It was such a nice warm autumn, and I was so engaged with the heifers and the grazing programs, and I had a lot of work with students on thesis requirements. I was oblivious, I guess."

"I think we've done all we can do here today. What do you have on for the rest of the weekend?"

"Depends on whether I can get a date for tonight at the last minute. What are your plans?"

"None so far. I could probably make myself available if you had any interest."

She stood up and came over and stood in front of him. "If it wouldn't be too hard on you, why don't we have a little sex before dinner, and then we can grill up a couple of Angus steaks and finish the salad and wine we never got to last night."

25

Woodpile

Kathryn and Herring had spent an hour in bed. Sex first, then they fell asleep for fifteen or twenty minutes, woke up, talked a bit, got up and took showers, and cooked the steaks. To both of them, it was as comfortable as if they had been together for months, not days. Perhaps it was because neither felt they needed to prove anything. They were who they were, and neither was likely to change greatly at this stage in their lives.

While he was showering, Herring thought how unlike one of the James Bond movies this was. Where Bond seduced the lesbian flight school owner and turned her back into a heterosexual lover of men. In this case, he was the one who had been seduced. That was all well and good. He wasn't sure he would have had the nerve to move forward. And if Kathryn someday wanted to tell him more about former partners and lovers, that would be fine. It would also be fine if it never came up.

After dinner, he drove home. They had decided to drive back out to see Douglas on Sunday at noon. Kathryn wanted to fill him in on what she had learned that week since the earlier visit, and Herring wanted to get to know him a bit better. Herring drove over to meet her around eleven thirty and they once again took her pickup. She had gone shopping for some grocery items for Douglas at the large supermarket in town. Mainly flour and yeast, concentrated milk, some dried fruits and beans, celery and carrots and onions. She explained that Douglas would make soups in batches on the wood-fired stove and then can them, depending on the season and the weather, and store them in the spring house he had built up behind his cabin. He had built a room out of stone with two steps down into a pool that was fed by a spring that ran all year. The water was always the same temperature and cold enough to keep even milk from going bad. The room was closed off so that bears and other animals couldn't get in and pee or defecate in the water. Douglas could drink it without worrying about the trichinosis that bears still carry. He still filtered it through a ceramic filter, but that probably was excessive.

The drive over was pleasant. The deciduous trees had now lost almost all of their leaves. The pines along the road were still showing signs of the damage from the Pine bark beetles that have ravaged the West, and now much of the East. Herring didn't know the history of the forests on this side of the valley but assumed that they had been damaged to the same degree as those on the other side of the valley, on the Blue Ridge chain that ran from Roanoke up to Front Royal. Most of the old-growth forest had been cut down long ago for fuel to supply the many miniature kilns that burnt the limestone to make lime, or to process the iron ore that was mined in small amounts all over the hills. There were individual holdings of twenty thousand acres or more that had been practically denuded by 1910. By that time, it was estimated that somewhere between one tenth of one percent and one percent of the trees on the entire East Coast was all that remained of the old-growth timber. Must have looked very different when the Europeans first arrived.

It was another unusually warm day for late November, a continued reminder that global warming was real. The high would be close to sixty degrees by three o'clock. A weather system from the south had pumped warm air and humidity up into the valley, and the day felt more like spring than fall, except for the naked forest all around them.

When they got to the road to Douglas's place they went through the usual procedure, and Herring helped Kathryn carry the bags of groceries up to the house. Douglas was behind the house, splitting logs with the help of a wedge and a sledge-hammer and a heavy axe for the small cuts. The wood itself had been cut to length with a chain saw. Douglas was shirtless but wore jeans and heavy boots and strong leather work gloves. When he spotted them, he set the axe with a blow into the chopping block and pulled off his gloves.

"Sheriff, you are screwed, my man. Well and truly screwed. Less than a week and you have been domesticated by my sister. Holy crap. And you don't even look unhappy about it. Carrying groceries. Driving out to the boonies to check on crazy brother. Have you set a date yet?"

Kathryn went up to Douglas and slapped him playfully on the cheek. "You never stop being a shit. You know that? Maybe he came to arrest you. Then we can set a different type of date."

Douglas smiled at Kathryn and then at Herring, but Herring would have sworn that Douglas's smile changed to an almost imperceptible flinch for just a moment at the word arrest. Not enough to indicate anything, and most likely a reflex based on his suspicion of all authority these days.

They took the groceries into the house, and Douglas offered them tea. "Kathryn was telling me about your spring house as we were driving over," said Herring. "We had one on the farm when I was growing up. Wonderful. There aren't many around anymore. Even if there were you couldn't use them with all of the ag chemicals on the crops."

"Oh that's for sure. Even up here in the woods, the acid rain affects the spring water. One of the few things I do trust in your world is water tests. I send some off occasionally. Especially in dry years."

"And…"

"Mineral content changes a little, but the spring stays clean. Of course, if someone starts logging near here or sprays for pine beetles I may be screwed. I own to the top and some distance on both sides, but I don't own the whole mountain.

"So, what news do we have for the week? I assume you two didn't come out here just to watch me chop wood."

"No, there are no answers but there is a bit more news." Kathryn took him through the high points, most of which involved the trust and prenup.

Douglas listened without interrupting until she finished with the summary. Then he looked her in the eye. "I would never have expected father to protect me. He never did. But to sell you out, to attempt to, is unforgivable. For that bitch. And that family. I'm going to need you both to go in a minute. I need to work through this. For those people, that family, and all that he wouldn't do for our mother. I need to focus that axe on that woodpile for a bit."

"Douglas, I'm sorry, I didn't mean to upset you so," said Kathryn, going to him and taking his hand. "It's okay now, I'll be fine. Things are like they were, the land is there, I have the cows and my house."

She looked at Herring, "And a new friend. A good friend."

Douglas looked at Herring. "I hope you are a good guy. I really do."

"There is one other thing," said Kathryn to Douglas. "Robert, Caroline's brother, the one who needed the money, is missing."

"Robert, the one who has his Klan robe custom-made at Brooks Brothers? That Robert? Missing as in how? Cradle-robbed a Confederate debutante from Ole Miss?"

"No, truly missing. Supposed to have shown up at a meeting in the Turks and Caicos about a money problem and never did."

"Well, I suppose he better hope his partners out there—which he must have since he isn't bright enough to put anything together more complicated than an order for a mint julep and some deviled eggs—are not members of the Mafia or a Mexican money-laundering investment group. If they are, I wouldn't set a place at the table for him any time soon."

"Douglas, I didn't like him, but I'm not sure I'd like him dead."

"Don't you get it? From what you just told me he is most likely the root of all that was about to be taken from you. I need to chop wood. Come back next Saturday. Bring the funeral notice for our esteemed father."

Herring was disappointed. As mercurial and strange as Douglas could be, he was still a person of incredible intelligence, and like no one he had ever met. Herring had enough of his grandfather's curiosity and respect for knowledge, that he would have liked to spend more time today talking to him. He wanted to learn more about the pixelated quilt he had been working on a few days ago.

Douglas had already gone back to the woodpile. Kathryn went out to use the composting toilet and Herring stood looking at and admiring the complete realm of Douglas's existence. Except for human companionship, which he apparently didn't want or require, he had everything a person needs. Electricity from a water turbine and the sun, water from the depths of the earth, heat from the wood of the trees around him, food mostly from the soil on the mountain. He was living a somewhat upgraded version of Native American life.

Maybe it was right to go off into the wild. It wasn't Alaska or upriver in the Amazon forests, but he had locked himself away and established order on a miniature scale. Carefully cut pieces of pine for kindling, dried potpourri of needles and leaves that made a fire starter, precisely cut, dry oak and poplar that would sustain the fire for hours, a tradition of coals to heat water, bake his bread and warm the house. And the quilts. Not to keep his body warm, but to keep his soul warm and alive. To keep his brain and psyche clear and focused. Douglas was probably right. The social media platforms that proliferated monthly—meant to bring people together—drove them apart and sent them into alienated states of depression instead. And the algorithms and the chips that he had helped to create, were now redefining humans as market units, objects to be measured and sold or sold to.

Kathryn returned and they set off down the mountain to her truck. Douglas ignored them as he positioned the chunks of log and readied them for the wedge and the axe.

26

Deep Thinker

Once they were through the gate and back on the road to Monterey, Herring asked Kathryn, "Do you think it's strange that your brother is more upset over Caroline's family trying to grab the money than he was over the death of your father?"

Kathryn was quiet for a moment as she thought it through. "In many respects, I would say no. Like I told you, Douglas values loyalty and trust. It's one of the traits of his spectrum. Extreme loyalty. I'm not sure, but I think he feels protective of me as maybe his only remaining connection with the human world. You know what I mean?"

"That's kind of scary. From his viewpoint I mean."

"Oh, for sure. It's like being the last man left on that planet in that movie a while back, if I'm gone."

"Even though he doesn't see you that much? And hardly ever leaves his compound?"

"Yeah, but I think that's enough. He does come over and stay at my house every few weeks if he knows father and Caroline will be gone. I think the fact of my existence and availability is a kind of lifeboat in his sea. He has otherwise given up on civilization. He told me a while back he was glad I never decided to get married and have kids because what they would face was too terrible to contemplate. He called life on earth a dead civilization walking, you know, like it was on death row. He really has little hope for the planet."

"Wow, that's bleak."

"Very, but when I think about his intelligence compared to the rest of us, even with his spectrum issues, I have to wonder if he isn't right. When he settles down, you should talk to him. He has thought it through very completely. Everything from global warming to people migrating, from mass communications to populism. He's very much in the *1984* camp of a totalitarian end view."

"That's even bleaker. I'm not overly optimistic, but I keep thinking that when push comes to shove, society will respond and try to fix things. Maybe that's too simple-minded on my part."

"Douglas would say it is. Not trying to insult you."

"Well, I've never been labeled a deep thinker." He looked off into the woods. The sun was now at their backs and the slow turning of the planet would soon leave the valleys in darkness.

27

Domesticated

Herring and Kathryn spent much of the ride back to her house in silence, each reflecting on Douglas and his tenuous hold on the reality that surrounded him. It was not a new thought for Kathryn because of her years with Douglas, but for Herring it was disquieting to think that all of a day's waking thoughts could potentially be taken up with such bleakness.

They decided not to spend the night together. Kathryn would have an early morning with moving cows again, and Herring needed to get home and rake the last of his leaves and finish putting his garden to bed for the winter.

Around noon, Herring came in from the garden to find that Berry had called. He called him back, and Berry answered immediately.

"What's up?" asked Herring.

"Lot's, maybe. Some very interesting information on young Bland. Guess where his cell phone last put him?"

"No idea, Siberia? Uruguay?"

"Just southwest of Staunton, Virginia. And the last transmission was Friday, November 24th around 5:00 p.m., the time Ashby and Caroline were probably killed."

"I'm stunned. How did he get there? What do the cell records show?"

"We have more. We pulled credit card charges. He flew into Richmond the night before from Turks and Caicos by way of Miami. He didn't get in until almost midnight. Presumably he spent the night at his place in Williamsburg. He has a house there on the river. He must not have had a car at the airport because he rented a MINI from Avis and it is still checked out. We checked with Avis in Richmond to see if they had GPS tracking but they claim not. So we don't know where the car is now. Or where Robert is."

"So, do you think *he* killed Ashby and his sister? That doesn't make any sense. If he killed Ashby or either one for that matter, he's now out of luck on getting any money. Unless Caroline had money squirreled away and he got it in her will. This makes no sense."

"I agree. It doesn't make sense for him to have killed them. It doesn't make sense for him to have sent the coffins. It doesn't make sense for him to disappear like that. It immediately casts him as guilty of the murders. It would have made more sense to establish an alibi. And not many people have the presence of mind to shut off their cell phones to avoid being tracked. Especially not if you are most likely panicked and trying to figure out what to do next. I have no idea."

"So what do we do?"

"You talk to Kathryn and see if she knows anything more. And tell her what we know, of course. And see if she ever saw him around the farm. I assume not, or she would have mentioned it."

"I think she would have. She told me she had only met him a few times. She despised him."

"What a mess. We will be in touch with the parents to see what they know. What a can of worms. Let me know if you learn anything." He clicked off.

Herring immediately called Kathryn and told her the news. "That's scary. If he really did do it, do you think he might come after me or Douglas?"

"I don't know. You haven't seen him around, right?"

"No, I don't know if he's been to the farm in the last ten years, more than the few times I've mentioned. He could have been here when I was away, but he hasn't been when I was around, and I didn't see him in the last two weeks."

"Okay, I think we should stick close together for the next few days, at least," suggested Herring.

"Someone to watch over me?" she asked. "That was a movie a long time ago. New York. Wealthy woman and a detective. Hmm. But he was married. And I'm not that wealthy. But you can still keep an eye on me. Do you think we should warn Douglas?"

"I don't know. If we had any idea of Robert's whereabouts, that would answer the question. I honestly think that if he planned to hurt you or Douglas, he would have tried by now. But that would only have compounded the risk to himself. And what would he gain? He must know there's no money to be had by now."

"If it works for you, can you go back with me tomorrow after lunch? To Monterey? And stay here tonight? I guess I'm kind of overusing the sheriff's department, aren't I? And the sheriff." In spite of the seriousness of the underlying threat, she was maintaining an irreverent sense of humor.

"We serve and protect."

"Bullshit, that's the Chicago motto."

"It's the sentiment that counts. I'll see you later this afternoon."

The new information added an additional layer of confusion to the already almost incomprehensible set of circumstances. Nothing tied together in terms of execution. Motive was certainly there on several levels, but the messages were mixed. And opportunity was now in the picture but seemed too happenstance. Herring decided to take the afternoon to do research and get his thoughts in order.

He drove to the office and logged into the computer there. He had decided to go back to the beginning and re-examine the first elements of the case. His first search was for pine coffins. He was surprised to find dozens of companies all over the US offering coffins and caskets of all types and sizes. He located several "Casket Builder" mail order companies that shipped kits and complete caskets to do-it-yourselfers, apparently.

They reported shipping hundreds of units per year and one site was backordered. It had never occurred to him that this market existed. He made a list of the half dozen most likely candidates in the eastern US and copied off email addresses and phone numbers. He would start calling tomorrow.

He had long ago given up on finding the source of the mannequins but decided to go the same route. In this case there were so many options that he gave up. Sites recommended dumpster diving behind stores that were going out of business, getting them through a Freecycle network, on Craig's list, or from discounters or eBay. Endless options and not enough time to explore them all.

He closed down the computer. Before he headed home to pick up a change of clothes and toiletries, he had the foresight to call Kathryn and ask if she needed him to pick up anything for dinner from any of the stores in town. She didn't, but he realized that brother Douglas might have been closer to the mark than he knew. He may have been domesticated in less than a week.

As he was leaving, he glanced at Blaine's word for the day. It was *modicum*, meaning a moderate or small amount. He decided that that word defined exactly the amount of knowledge he had of the case.

28

Paydirt

Herring returned to the office at 7:00 a.m. He sent a secure email to Berry asking him to look at Robert Bland's credit card bills for any charges from coffin or casket makers or mannequin suppliers.

At eight he called Blaine and Roddie into his office and spent a minute catching up on some light personal stuff with them. He confessed to Blaine that he takes a look at the word-of-the-day calendar before leaving the office most days. And that recent words had seemed especially applicable to his own circumstances. Roddie's wife had kept him busy all weekend winterizing the windows and doors with weather stripping, cutting firewood, raking leaves. Herring gave them as much of an update as he could. He asked that they keep an eye out for the rental car, a MINI. He printed out a photo that Berry had sent of Robert for identification in case Robert was holed up somewhere. Herring put the odds of that near zero.

He then got on the phone. On the third call he hit possible paydirt at Casket Builder Supply. He learned that someone had ordered six kits in early September. She remembered the order because it was a large order. Most people ordered only one or two. It was a new customer who claimed to be a small under-taker. She had never heard the name before, but he seemed to not want to provide details. She remembered hoping it wasn't some gang member planning to kill a bunch of people. Finally, the customer insisted on paying with a money order, which was unusual, and wanted the caskets shipped to a FedEx depot in Richmond to be held for pick up. The customer had given a phone number. She had called, as a courtesy to tell him that she had received the money order and the kits would go out the next day. But there had been no answer. The kits were shipped as requested.

Herring ended the call. A Richmond delivery put the caskets close to Williamsburg and Robert, but he couldn't see Robert assembling them and setting up the scenes. From what he'd heard, Robert didn't sound like the DIY type. What he could see though, was that the transaction was untraceable. They would get copies of the money order, but a sender does not need to sign a postal money order. That would tell them nothing except where it had been bought. The lady at the casket company was going to pull the shipping file and scan the documents and send them to sheriff's office.

Herring called Berry and filled him in. He asked Berry to have someone from the Richmond office go to the FedEx location and see what they could learn. If anyone remembered a pickup of a large order from almost three months earlier, he would be stunned. It appeared likely that the mannequins could have been ordered, paid for, shipped, and collected in the same way. In a world where everything was traceable and every customer identifiable, suddenly this wasn't the case.

29

Goat's Milk

Herring left the office a little before noon, picked up a couple of BLTs on sourdough toast for the ride to Douglas's. He also ordered some fries to munch on during his twenty-minute drive to Kathryn's. They used his pickup this time, and by one thirty were through the gate and walking up to Douglas's house. There was no sign of him at first. The woodpile from the day before had changed dimensions, with far fewer chunks to be split and a large pile of split pieces ready to be ricked for further drying. Douglas must have worked off a lot of anger over the past twenty hours.

Herring and Kathryn walked around the house to the sunnier southwest side and peered in. No sign of him inside. They headed up to the spring house on a narrow footpath that led past a stone dam and the little water turbine. They opened the heavy wooden door that protected the spring house and found a row of jars of soups, and some glass containers that looked like they held yogurt.

"I forgot about that," said Kathryn. "Douglas gets milk from a lady with some goats just down the valley and makes his own yogurt. It's an overnight deal with a little heater thing he has and some starter. He eats yogurt with his own homemade muesli every morning. Maybe he went to get the milk. I think he bikes down and picks it up the first of every week. I forgot about that."

"How far away is it?"

"Not far, I think maybe five miles. I've never been there."

"So he does get out in the community and ride his bike? That makes more sense than almost never leaving here."

"I don't think he goes far, but it is a change."

They closed and fastened the door that kept the animals out, and also probably kept the temperature more even. Herring had noted that the short roof trusses were set flush into the top of the wall and plastered in so that no animals, like raccoons or snakes could get in under the eaves. In addition, where the water exited the building through a stone channel, Douglas had cemented into place a stainless-steel grid that kept anything from entering from that direction. His design was meticulous in all areas, leaving nothing to chance.

When they got back down to the house, Douglas was just coming around the corner wearing a backpack that looked heavy. He saw them and continued to the back door, took out a key, opened it and disappeared inside. The backpack held two large glass jars wrapped in a kind of woven caning, something like old French wine bottle carriers. Each had a resealable cork top.

"Nectar of the goats," said Douglas. "Were you just up at the spring?"

"Yes," said Kathryn and gave him a hug which he half-heartedly returned. "How are you today?"

"I *was* pretty good but I'm not so sure now. Why are you back so soon? Did Caroline come back to life or something and we still have to put up with the bitch?"

"Douglas, we just came to tell you to keep an eye out. Redd, will you tell him?"

Herring explained that Robert's cell phone had shown him to be at the farm at about the time of the killings and that he had rented a car in Richmond when he was supposed to have been in the Turks. Even though it was remote, they just wanted to warn him that Robert might still be looking to harm him or Kathryn.

"It seems a little late for that, don't you think?" said Douglas. "I would have thought he would have gone after one of us by now if he was going to. Where were you when all of this was happening?" he asked Kathryn.

"Camping, north of here as a matter of fact. I told you. I ate bad mushrooms and went back early and found the plane."

"Oh, that's right. Well, I'm glad you are safe. And sheriff, in spite of what I said, I really do appreciate you looking after my baby sister here. She is the only close person who never betrayed me. I value that very highly."

That statement moved Herring, but it also caused him to wonder what lengths Douglas would go to protect Kathryn if he found her in danger. He was unwilling to ask it at this point, because it seemed unnecessary. But he filed the thought away. He also wondered why Douglas hadn't remembered where Kathryn was the day of the murder. He didn't recall hearing her tell him on the first trip, but he hadn't been with them all of the time. As he processed this thought another one slipped in. He had never verified where Kathryn had camped or asked her to take him there. He had never tried to verify if she really had been sick from mushrooms. And an even worse thought slipped in. Surely Kathryn and Douglas could not have killed Ashby and Caroline and covered their actions? Kathryn had been genuinely surprised to learn what her father was planning. If she had known before, she would have confronted him and probably could have stopped it. And Douglas almost never went anywhere but to her house rarely and to the goat farm weekly. He would have had to make multiple trips out to order and buy the coffins and mannequins, to stage them, to send the warnings. It was not possible. He processed that and put it away. It was unthinkable.

"Since we drove all the way out here, what's new in the past week? How's progress on the quilt?" asked Kathryn.

"Slow, I had to re-dye some colors. Hidden stitching is always a bear, but it makes the cloth look like the paint dabs. You can go look at it. It's going to be a while before it's done."

Herring spoke up. "Well, I could never do anything this complicated anyhow, but if I could, it would certainly not be something that only I would ever see."

"Well, I told you earlier, me and God. The beauty of the planet, the beauty of the universe at night and nothing but a bunch of dinosaurs and giant worms to inhabit it. No appreciation for the world around them. Then some humans get let in. Bad mistake. It's been downhill for the earth ever since. Better left unobserved and unappreciated. There was some philosopher who said that the very act of looking at an object changed it. So don't go frowning at my quilt."

Herring and Kathryn both smiled at that comment. Douglas had a quirky sense of humor.

They stayed for another hour and talked a bit about how Douglas did things. Making yogurt, where the dishwater drained to, how the Native Americans had managed the woods and valleys, the fact that Douglas had seen foxes frequently and maybe a bobcat. The smaller number of birds migrating each year. Fortunately, there were no feral hogs that he knew of, animals that were decimating the forests in places in the South and lower Midwest. Herring and Kathryn left around three.

When they got back to the farm at around five, it was starting to get dark. Herring went with Kathryn to check some heifers a mile from the house. They had been spooked by a fox or a skunk a few days earlier and she wanted to see that they were comfortable and had enough hay and grass. Herring thought it might be more a of a ritual for her to see the animals and wish them good night, than any substantial concern for feed or pests.

They also stopped by the main house to see that all was well, and that no one had tried to break in. There was a pile of mail in the mailbox, and they took that with them back to Kathryn's. Herring called the dispatcher, and there was nothing that needed his attention for the evening. Berry had not called on the special phone during the afternoon.

They were both tired from the activities of the day. Kathryn had some frozen stew that she thawed, and they ate it with a bit of leftover baguette and the remains of salad greens and some cucumber that was near the end of its shelf life. They made a fire in the fireplace, and both read through the emails from the attorneys one more time to see what had been missed. A few supporting documents had come in to Kathryn's email from the attorneys. She printed them and they looked them over. Nothing that changed any part of what they already knew.

Herring stayed and they went to bed at ten, made love slowly, and fell asleep afterward. They didn't wake until five thirty the next morning. Kathryn had to meet with the herdsmen before she could head to Charlottesville for the meeting with the accountants. Herring was going along, so he went home to change into something more businesslike.

30

Accountants

The office of the accounting firm of Elder, Buckner, and Warren was located on old Highway 250 West, a postcolonial design certainly inspired by Jeffersonian tradition. The brass plate on the front of the building noted that the firm had been established in 1955. There were twelve names on a separate shield, those of eleven men and one woman. Elder and Buckner were at the top of the list and noted as founders. If they were still active in the firm, they would both be over ninety. Double-entry bookkeeping had been around forever, but the tax codes were almost all new.

Herring had decided to dress in what has become known as business casual. He had on grey slacks, a pale blue and yellow tattersall shirt, and a navy-blue blazer that had been his go-to for years. His shoes were cordovan plain-toe bluchers he had bought on sale at Allen Edmonds. His wife had been a sensible and knowledgeable dresser and had taught him how to dress affordably, in a classic manner that befitted his role as a professional.

Kathryn was wearing black wool slacks, a white silk blouse, and a beautifully tailored grey wool tweed jacket. Her soft black leather loafers with a tan trim had a stapled pearl design around the toe. They looked like a luxury brand. Herring wondered if they were Italian. When he picked her up at her house, he told her he looked like her chauffeur with his blazer. But she just laughed at him and told him he looked like old money.

They were greeted by a middle-aged receptionist seated behind a large antique reproduction cherry desk. There were wing chairs and an inviting lounge sofa arranged in front of a non-working fireplace to her right. But they were immediately shown instead into a conference room down an elegant hall. Leather side chairs surrounded a conference table that could seat a dozen or more. If it hadn't been for the plaque on the door, Herring might have thought they had wandered into a private executive board room, as opposed to an accountant's office.

The receptionist, who introduced herself as Mrs. Bargers, asked if they would like coffee or water, and said she would send in Mr. Becker, the partner in charge of the Ashby accounts. Kathryn had worked with him before. They accepted water and a moment later Ernest Becker, a slightly portly and greying man of about fifty-five whose eyebrows needed trimming, stepped into the room. He was accompanied by a younger man who was even more portly, but less gray, whom he introduced as Brad something, his assistant.

Hands were shaken, condolences issued, introductions acknowledged, and all were seated.

Kathryn began the conversation. "Ernest, I don't think you'll be surprised to hear that I am not very happy to learn, at this late date, that you were working with my father to restructure, apparently, most of the business interests without my knowledge. I thought you worked for both of us."

Becker responded without seeming to have taken her mood into account. "I do apologize, but the fact is that your father was addressing only those segments of the business that applied directly to his ownership and we have confidentiality agreements in place."

Kathryn held up her hand and stopped him. "Ernest, that sounds like bullshit to me. Any one part of the farm affected all the rest of it, and you had a responsibility to inform me."

"But Kathryn, we hadn't done anything yet, and didn't even have a concrete plan. You would have been informed and would have had to agree to some of the ideas and items. You have to understand two things. One, Mr. Ashby told us he wanted to be the one to discuss it with you when it came time, and he didn't want us to be involved with you until that time. Second, he told us he was only exploring options and might not even go through with them, and he didn't want to cause you worry in case he decided not to change anything."

"I might accept that explanation, but I'm not sure. Why don't you lay out what my father was up to, and let me make up my own mind?"

"Yes, gladly. I'm sorry for the misunderstanding. Here are the basics." At that point he asked for a folder from Brad, who had been glancing back and forth uncomfortably between the two of them as they talked.

"First of all, Mr. Ashby wanted us to look at options relative to use of cash or equity in the aircraft venture. That took a bit of time. It turns out that while the government-related work has been a good cash provider for the company, there are several other segments that have not. And while the business has been profitable overall, it is barely so at this time. There apparently was a problem with a plane purchase from somewhere in Africa. While the planes have been paid for, or at least the money is out in escrow, there was a reshuffle in government. Someone wants a fee to expedite the transaction and as you probably know, that is illegal under US law. It will probably get resolved soon, but it turns out his partners in the company don't have the excess funds to buy out your father at this time."

"But he did have the use of the plane, as it turns out?'

"Yes, he had essentially a no cost lease and he just paid fuel and maintenance and so forth. It was a part of his compensation, and he had to pay taxes on the fair market value of his use."

"What about the farm and the prenup and the trust and all of that? What was he trying to do?"

"Well, it's quite complex and that's why we hadn't gotten very far. The prenup and the revocable generation skipping trust are documents that only he had control over. So we could not have involved you in those discussions. What he initially wanted to do was borrow money against the value of the items in the trust, primarily the land and the house and facilities and so on. He did not mention selling anything. Under the terms of the trust, he had every right to do that. The problem arose when the banks he has worked with required personal guarantees and cross-collateralization. You know what that means of course."

"Yes, he was personally responsible, not just the corporation. And the collateralization means everything guarantees everything else and is liable for the debts. But did that extend to the cattle business we own jointly?"

"Yes and no. It was not a part of the cross-collateral agreements, or you would have had to sign. But it could have been construed as part of the personal guarantee, unless his attorneys got the bank to let him exempt it. I can't answer you on that."

"Well, it's beside the point now. More importantly, what was he planning to do with the money he wanted to borrow, to your knowledge?"

"I'm surprised this never came up. He said he was keeping you apprised. He planned to loan it to a real estate venture that his wife's family was involved in that needed temporary cash to make it through a transition period. He was planning to set up a separate LLC to hold the money and lend it out."

"Were you setting up that LLC?"

"No, he was working with the family on that. We were just investigating the accounting issues. We were waiting for the attorneys to untangle the rest. In lots of ways what he was doing was not that unusual. Almost all of the trusts that we work with do transactions like this constantly. The trusts just hold the assets of normal functioning businesses that carry on as usual. It mostly just involves more papers to sign."

"So where are we now?"

"Where we always would have been in case of a natural death. The land stays in the trust. The rent paid by the cattle business continues to cover the mortgage until the mortgage is retired. Once the mortgage is retired, the rent from the cattle business gets invested back into the farm or paid out according to the terms. I think you get half after taxes, the other half would have gone to Caroline, but now just accumulates."

"And the cattle business?"

"Unless there was a change in the will we don't know about, you inherit his portion and there may be some tax to pay, but the inheritance tax levels have been raised so it all depends on how the cattle are valued. You probably won't have much to pay. And that business is all yours now."

"I am having a hard time with all of it. From the death to what he was plotting. I don't get it."

"Well, Miss Ashby, we don't either. I hope whoever did this is found and punished. I apologize again for our not being able to discuss any of the other business with you, but that is a moot point as far as I know now."

"Yes, one thing led to another. Redd, do you have any questions from a legal or investigation standpoint?"

"No, I'm not up to snuff on all of the accounting and tax stuff. But the FBI is involved in this Mr. Becker, and they will probably want to review some of it. I don't suppose there is anyone else who was involved in your discussions that you haven't mentioned is there?"

"No, no one that we were involved with. As I told you, Mr. Ashby was planning to set up a separate LLC with the family firms. The only thing he mentioned was that he wanted to end the personal guarantees and the cross-collateralization agreements and that he was discussing that with an insurance company or a private equity group from Florida. From a personal standpoint, I can tell you that that would have been a bad idea. Those groups would have charged probably double the interest he was paying on remaining debt at the moment for that privilege. Maybe 8 percent or so, when he was paying only 4.5 now on the old mortgage. I presume he would have then loaned it out at an even higher rate."

"Strange, increasing risk and exposure when you don't need to. Thanks for your help."

When the meeting ended Kathryn suggested lunch in town and they went to a little place near the old train station for a quiche and salad. Herring's life was indeed getting upgraded.

31

Thumb Drive

They were back at the farm by 2:00 p.m. Herring dropped Kathryn at her house and went to the office to check in with his deputies and see if they had learned anything that would advance the case. Blaine was finishing up notes on a bank robbery attempt. The FBI has authority over bank robbery investigations, but in practice, local authorities usually do the investigations, especially if the amounts are small. In this case, the bank teller, a former high school teacher, had recognized the robber as one of her former students, even with his mask. The would-be robber didn't realize who he was talking to until she called him out. He ran from the bank and the sheriff's department was still looking for him.

Herring was about to call Berry when his cell phone rang. It was Kathryn. "You need to get out here right away."

Herring was rising from his seat as she spoke. "What, what's happening? Are you okay?"

"I'm fine, I'm fine, but I found something. In one of the barns. I'll explain it when you get here. It's a thumb drive for a computer. I ran home and opened it on my laptop. I only looked at a couple of things, but it must be from my father's laptop. There are pictures, emails, a bunch of stuff."

"Alright, I'm on the way. Are you sure you should access it?"

"It's too late—I already did. I saved it onto my laptop."

"Do we need to let Berry see it?"

"Let's see what all is on it first. Then I can make a file and send it to him if he needs it. Just get here and look at it with me."

Herring left immediately and was there in twenty minutes. Kathryn's truck was in the driveway and the gate was open to the patio. He went in and found her hunched over her laptop. At her direction, he pulled a chair around beside her and sat down.

"Let me go back to the beginning so you understand the sequence and what I'm seeing."

"Wait, first things first. Where did you find this?"

"It was in one of the back barns. You've never been there. I went over to use the Bobcat and load out a couple of bales of hay. When I was sliding the prongs up to the first bale, I saw something shiny just as I lifted the bale. It looked like it had fallen between the bales or gotten shoved under and in the gap. There's always loose hay on the ground around the bales, so it was hidden. That shed is usually locked, and it was locked when I got there because we keep a Bobcat loader there. Anyway, there was one more thing. We store a lot of hay in those white plastic wrappers. Outdoors in a lot behind that barn, someone had cut one of the wrappers off."

"I'd like to see that, but later. Let's see what you have here."

It turned out to be a treasure trove from one angle. Like all the info so far, it raised more questions than it answered. It was almost a library of documents from the last three months. The first documents were grainy photos taken in northern Iraq, most likely. They showed almost exactly what Berry had discussed the previous week. There were at least four dead bodies, all Iraqi. One was a boy with a horrible neck injury that had almost severed his head. Another was a woman with a baby tied to her bosom, and both had been shot through. There was another body of indeterminate age and Ashby was standing over it. He was not in the other two photos. Kathryn looked at Herring as he examined the photos.

"Berry told me there was some bad stuff out there, but I had no idea. I'm sorry you have to see this."

"You knew?"

"Please, don't get upset with me. I have never seen these, and Berry told me these were acts covered under military secrecy and he didn't know if the events were even real, or made up, or even related to Ashby."

"You know, a lot of people have kept a lot of stuff from me over the past couple of weeks. There better not be much more." She was clearly upset, but Herring felt he had been right not to talk about it before now.

He put his hand on her arm, but she shook it off. "Let's get to more of what's in here."

The next set of photos was of the coffins that had been placed in the area in the weeks leading up to the murder. All were of the exact locations. All of them had been printed and scanned or scanned from originals or so it appeared from the shading.

Next was a set of emails. Each was dated. Herring pulled out his phone. In each case the email had been sent the day the coffin had been discovered.

Herring looked closely at all of the emails. He noted that the sender in each case was a slightly different set of numbers @protonmail.ch. He had no idea what that was, but Kathryn did.

"It's the dark web, encrypted emails. Almost impossible to trace the sender, although I imagine the government could."

"So we have a set of incriminating photos from Iraq, staged scenes of parts of those actions photographed and sent to your father, and messages that must have meant something to him but not to the rest of us. Whoever had the photos from Iraq must have been with him there or had access to the photos and used them to send a warning. This looks like blackmail."

"It doesn't seem like something Robert would be capable of or would know enough about. But it feels like too much of a coincidence for Robert to need the money, while someone from Ashby's Iraqi past was warning him about some other undefined action that they wanted stopped. This makes no sense."

Kathryn picked up the thumb drive that had been setting by the computer. "I wonder if my father was going to hand this over to someone in DC, to see if they could figure out who was at the root of this? Maybe that's why he and Caroline had left so early. It's pretty concise."

"That could make sense. But why did they come back to the farm unexpectedly that day? These emails have to tie directly to their death. Your father and Caroline were put in coffins exactly like the ones used to warn him. I wonder if there were other emails that he didn't want on this drive. Maybe he wanted someone in DC to see who was harassing him but wanted to keep something else secret. You remember our discussion? That we wouldn't take something like the initial coffin as much more than a sick joke? I think maybe Robert got himself into a jam at just the wrong time.

"Clearly Ashby was working to get some money freed up to help Robert out, but someone from his military past had another idea. If they could get into your father's computer and look at his emails, and if they were sending stuff on this dark web, they probably could hack it. They may have been alarmed that he was going to give away money that they wanted from him. It still doesn't explain why whoever killed him, killed him. Unless they met him here that day and he point blank refused and they decided to kill him out of anger and revenge."

Kathryn sat thinking for a moment. "Maybe we're just being stupid here. Maybe none of this has anything to do with some terrorist or revenge group. Maybe this was all done by Robert's partners. We have no idea who those guys are. We don't even know if they are from the US. It sounds more like the things South American drug guys or Russian mobsters would resort to." She paused, then continued. "I wonder where the hell Robert is. If what I just said is right, maybe he felt he was in danger and disappeared somewhere. I think you better get your guy Berry to get to working on this. Can I just email him something, or is he buried in some dark website himself?"

"I don't know. I'll call him. I think you can just send it to some secure location."

Herring called Berry and was given a secure email address where incoming mail was screened for viruses and all the other intrusive hacker elements before being printed and deleted. It turned out paper was sometimes the best barrier to incursion after all.

Herring returned to his office. Another dimension had been added to the case, and he felt like he was further from an answer than ever before. He did, however, feel relieved that most of what he had seen and read pointed away from Kathryn and Douglas, and toward Robert and either his investment group, or some sinister interests from back in Ashby's past. He fleetingly pondered whether the two could be the same but rejected that as much too far out there to be a possibility.

Most of his cases were nowhere near this intellectually chal- lenging. There had been only one murder in the past year not counting these. There had been a number of assaults but mostly crimes related to property same as the rest of the country. And people knew their neighbors and kept an eye out for things out of the ordinary. The upside to this, he had to admit, was getting to know Kathryn. He so hoped that nothing turned up that would threaten that. He also realized that if it did, his career as sheriff would be over. It would be a humiliating end.

Roddie was at the office, about to depart for home. "Roddie, I appreciate you and Blaine covering for me while we sort this coffin murder business out. I think it was always going to be over our heads with the colonel and his international connections. It's usually a pissed-off relative that does it around here."

Roddie looked at him. "What makes you think it isn't this time, Sheriff? Maybe you're just making it too complicated. See you tomorrow. I'll bring in some pie. Wife kind of overdid the baking."

Herring said goodbye, but the comment had served to bring his worries back to the surface.

Before leaving he stepped over to Blaine's desk to look at the word for the day. It was *irenic*, which meant to promote peace or understanding, peaceful or conciliatory. He was pretty sure he had never heard that word before, and it was the opposite of what had driven the events of the past several months out at the farm.

32

The Blands

Herring spent the night at home but did not sleep well. He called Kathryn at eight in the evening. They spoke for a few minutes, but both were tired from the trip to Charlottesville and the stress of the meeting, as well as from the trove of emails. He also felt guilty on two counts. For one, he should never have become involved with Kathryn while an investigation was going on. It was a singular firing offense. He had put her in the role of victim but with no evidence to support that theory. On the second count, he felt guilty for not standing by her and protecting her in case Robert or some group related to him, or to someone in her father's past, still would attempt to harm her. It seemed unlikely at this late stage, but in truth, they knew so little about what had really happened that his beliefs were of little value.

He checked in with her again at seven in the morning. It was now Thursday and instead of the actual thirteen days since the finding of the bodies, it seemed like a month. He had not updated his checklist on events but planned to do so this morning when he got to the office. As it turned out, that would have to wait.

The phone Berry gave him was buzzing in his pocket as he rolled into the parking lot. He pulled into his space, pulled out the phone, and clicked it on.

With no greeting, Berry started in. "I am sending you a secure email with a lot of details. There will be instructions on how to open it. Here are the basics. We still haven't found the rental car that Caroline's brother picked up in Charlottesville. He just disappeared after his cell phone shut off at the farm. There is no cell phone signal that shows him or the phone in the car after the 4:30 p.m. time of the murders.

"That's point one. Second, we have, with the help of the Blands, or at least Mr. Bland, found out a bit more about the Turks and Caicos venture. Bland was pretty blustery and defensive for a bit until we told him that the death of his daughter, the disappearance of his son, and what appeared to be financial irregularities were not joking matters. That if he had been involved in any of it, he could be culpable. Bullshit, all of it, but he really irritated me with his southern tradition claptrap. Anyway, he finally admitted that he had not been totally comfortable with the Turks deal and had not put much of his own money in. He and Robert had worked with a small group of investors over the years to buy or occasionally build a few small apartment complexes around Raleigh and Atlanta and mid-south cities. All small-time easily managed things.

"But Robert had started to hang out with people in Miami and had gotten sucked into the idea of investing in a condo resort in Turks. Bland had advised against it. He had not liked the people Robert introduced him to. He may be an asshole, but I don't think he is all that dumb. He has about a five million dollars net worth from what our financial people can see and clears about three hundred and fifty thousand dollars after tax most years.

"At any rate, Robert got into the deal with a smaller amount of cash than Bland senior thought was legitimate. He thinks that Robert may have been used as the front person to help launder money for the other partners. He doesn't know what Robert promised or any details. But Robert came to him after the hurricane and wanted to borrow a lot of money. The Turks investment group apparently held him responsible for not insuring the project properly, which really wasn't his fault, I don't imagine. But hey, they wanted money to cover the damages or investments or whatever.

"I asked Bland if Robert might have overrepresented his ability to pay or play and he said yes, unfortunately that could have been the case."

"Lord, I thought this was complicated before. So apparently the Turk group could have been behind all of what was going on up in Augusta County? That sounds too roundabout to me. Why not just threaten Ashby?"

"Well, Ashby wasn't a party to any of this. He was the only person with the possibility of coming up with some cash, but it would have had to come through his wife. And maybe he just didn't want to cough up ten million dollars or whatever. So, someone cooked up a blackmail scheme to get at him. It's kind of a soft blackmail in a way, if you think about it. They needed the money, but presumably it was still someday going to be a solid investment for Ashby. So it wasn't like pouring it down a rat hole to buy silence. Or at least that's the way you could position it."

"What happened? At this point it looks like Robert met with Ashby and Caroline, and instead of getting money he killed them and then he disappeared and no one is satisfied? Or do you have information that would say Robert didn't do this, or had help?"

"I don't. We've sent agents to Turks to check out the investment group. We are still looking at hotels near the airport in Charlottesville, of which there are almost none, and at flights

211

out the next day. Unless he used a different name, Robert didn't fly out of there. And he hasn't been back to his apartment in Williamsburg. He has just vanished.

"We are doing a background check on Robert now. There is nothing to indicate a tendency to be this violent. Once we see who he was tied up with in Turks, we may know more. There have been a lot of real estate investment schemes there, in the US, and all over the Caribbean that are basically money laundering investments. They're built to get a clean pedigree and then sold on. This fits that pattern. The hurricane just happened to short circuit this one. And people who need to launder money don't usually have a sense of humor. You would think that if you were a big-time drug dealer you would just accept the occasional loss or misfire as part of doing business and move on. But that has not been our experience with them. Every loss is personal and they either get it back or kill you. But I'm jumping ahead. We don't know yet."

"So what do you want me to do here in the valley?"

"I'm sending a couple of people out from Richmond. They should be there in an hour or so. Take them out to where Kathryn found the thumb drive and where you said the plastic was missing. And have them look at the barn by where the plane was parked. They will pull some more samples and see what we come up with. These are evidence specialists."

"Okay, have them meet me here. I'll go get the email and look at the details. We can talk later today. By the way, I've never been to Turks. Is it nice?"

"I guess so. I haven't either. But it's the rainy season down there right now. I guess it gets nice after Christmas."

"Later." Herring hung up. He sat in the truck for a few more minutes trying to get his thoughts in order. There were so many themes in this case, but instead of supporting each other they seemed to work at odds. Or if they did work in the same direction, they were at oblique angles. There was also something that he had seen in the past week that did not fit. It was something almost felt as opposed to being seen, but it kept creeping back like a title of a long-forgotten song. It wouldn't slip into place, and it made him uncomfortable to have that hanging there, along with all of the pieces of the newly much more complex puzzle.

True to Berry's estimate, the evidence specialists arrived forty-five minutes later. Herring had called Kathryn to tell her they were on the way, and they met at her house and then drove to the barn where she had found the missing plastic and the thumb drive. No one else had been in the barn, but the Bobcat had stirred up the chaff and dust and loose hay on the ground so the odds of finding footprints or other evidence seemed remote. Nevertheless, the technicians marked off the area that Kathryn pointed out by the big round bales and divided it into square-foot portions. They numbered them with plastic numbers like those found in some old restaurants where your number was called when your order was ready. They photographed the area and then carefully bagged the contents of each section and labelled them.

When this was done, they photographed the area around the round bales where the plastic had been cut away and looked for footprints or tire tracks. Here again the area had been disturbed by the Bobcat. The hay stored here was of a different type and had lower protein and was fed to the cows, while the indoor bales were alfalfa and went to the growing heifers. Here the technicians took photographs, but there was not much to gather but dust and chaff so nothing was bagged.

The next stop was at the hangar where the plane would have been stored normally, and where the final signals from Robert's cell phone ended. Presumably where Ashby and Caroline had been killed. Samples of stains on the floor had been taken the first time and had contained blood from both victims and some urine stains. The technicians this time did a more complete search of the building in hopes of finding the cell phone or any other traces of evidence they might have missed earlier. They used a high-end metal detector but located nothing but normal tools and supplies. One thing that was a mystery to everyone was why the bodies had been cleaned after the killing, and how many people it would have taken to do this.

The final stop for the forensics team was to look once more at the hospital area that was a part of one of the nearby barns. Cattle get sick and need to be given shots and occasionally they need to be put into small hospital pens indoors for special feed and treatments. There are specialized corrals and chutes that are used to hold them still for taking temperatures and giving shots. Because of the value of the cattle at Celebration farm, these facilities were of exceptionally high quality, better padded than most on a ranch, and the hospital was kept clean and disinfected. The walls and floor were washable and were cleaned and disinfected after each use. The area had been looked at after the killing, but it was clean and did not appear to have been used for anything other than cattle treatment. It had had the smell of the disinfectants generally used, as it did now, with an additional odor of cattle manure from two older calves penned up there for observation. Other calves had been through the hospital as well in the past ten days.

One of the technicians asked Kathryn where the wash down and waste went. She showed him the locations of the drains, which were routed through a screen and then to a soak-away constructed of stone some yards from the barn. It was agreed that nothing that would add evidence could be gained from further examination of the facility. One thing that Herring was noting, probably due to his farming background, was that there were enough Bobcats, loaders, winches, pulleys, and lifting devices all over the farm for a single individual to have handled the bodies, not easily, but adequately if necessary.

By noon the technicians had gathered all that they needed, and they departed for Richmond. Kathryn went back to moving heifers with the two herdsmen, and Herring went back to the office after stopping for a burger at Mike's.

33

The Matrix

At this point, Herring wanted to pull together all of the strings of the investigation to see if he could make any sense of it. He had been planning on doing this earlier but had been called away by the finding of the thumb drive.

When he got back to the office, he tore several sheets of paper off of a presentation pad in a conference room and took them into his office and closed the door.

He decided to create a matrix of victim, possible killer, and motive associated with that killer. He also wanted to put plusses and minuses in a category to establish some sort of probability:

Victim	Potential Killer	Motive	Probability	Evidence Strength
Colonel Ashby	Terrorist group	Revenge/ reparations	+	Moderate w/ warnings/coffins
	Robert Bland	money	++	circumstantial
	Bland's Turks partners	money	-	No evidence

Victim	Potential Killer	Motive	Probability	Evidence Strength
Colonel Ashby	Douglas Ashby	Protect Kathryn's interests	-	Potentially strong/source of knowledge of father's plans?
	Kathryn	Protect own livelihood	-	Unprovable alibi/ genuine surprise
Caroline Ashby	Collateral damage	Avenue for money from Ashby	- - -	
Robert Bland if dead?	Colonel		none	
	Terrorist group	none	- -	none
	Douglas	Protect Kathryn	-	none
	Kathryn	Protect self-interests	none	None, but with above caveat
	Turks partners	Frustration/ disillusion	-	None to date

Now that he had what he assumed to be the whole cast of characters on the board, he felt like he could begin to make better sense of the possibilities. It occurred to him once again that Douglas could maybe have just written some sort of algorithm that would sort the whole thing out, or at least spit out a probability number.

As Herring studied his matrix it came to mind that perhaps there were two segments to the puzzle that might not relate to each other directly. What if the coffin warnings had been sent by a terrorist group after all, with the intention of ruining Ashby's reputation? Perhaps as the only reasonable payback they could expect, operating from such a distance? They mentioned money in the emails, but perhaps they never really expected to collect, and would continue to send the macabre messages until they saw some sign that he was cowed? The problem was that they had gone to a lot of effort and substantial risk in ordering, assembling, and placing the coffins over the four- to six-week period. But who else could possibly have known about the atrocities unless Ashby had bragged about it? And it's not likely that he would have bragged to any of the other parties.

As to the second segment Herring was considering, what if the killings of Ashby and Caroline had nothing whatsoever to do with the coffin warnings? What if Robert was pushing his sister to get the changes made, and it seemed to be proceeding, but his partners became suspicious and impatient and pushed him to make things happen faster? What if Ashby, after starting the work on the prenup and trust agreements, decided not to go through with it? What if Robert threatened him and in a fit of anger killed both Ashby and his sister? Then disappeared so as not to be caught. But where would he go and what would he use for funds and how would he know how to disappear so completely? Douglas might know how to do that, but not Robert, he guessed. Which brought him back to that little something that he had felt or seen in the past week that kept haunting him.

He decided to craft a set of questions to fill in some of his blanks. He needed to start with Berry and a bit more information on Robert and the partnership.

Berry did not answer when Herring called. So he went back to his matrix and tried to build in the background that would have been necessary for all of the events to have happened in the way they did.

First, whoever had planned the coffin and mannequin warnings had to have a scheme that would get Ashby to react, either positively or negatively. What if the coffins had been a warning to Ashby to not go through with the changes to the prenup? The only two people who would have cared about that were most likely Douglas and Kathryn. Douglas because he wanted to protect his sister as the only person close to him who had not betrayed him, and because he genuinely admired her. But he would have had to come out of his hideaway and do some serious research on the internet on a timely basis, and then figure out a way to intimidate his father that did not involve direct contact. His father would not pay attention to a verbal warning or a plea from Douglas. That much seemed clear from what he had learned about the family.

The messages that had been on the thumb drive were asking for Ashby to stop the financial shenanigans and might next ask for money for Ashby's victims. Herring could see how closely the pictures and the emails were linked. It appeared they'd been sent as attachments. He wondered if there were more. Perhaps Ashby had selected the ones to put on the thumb drive, if he had been taking it to DC to hand over to someone to investigate. But with the laptop gone, they might never know. Still a wrinkle.

While Herring was thinking this through, his FBI phone rang. Berry was just back from a meeting and had some background.

"Our financial guys pulled up some interesting background, but I'm not sure it aids us much in finding Robert Bland Jr. Here's what they found. First, he *was* a necessary partner. In Turks, corporations can own buildings and condos and things like that but cannot own land. Only an individual can own land. We can guess that none of the other partners in this venture wanted their names on the land, so Robert was the one in the landowner role. The other partners, whom we have found all had entities domiciled in Panama, were only represented by counsel, and all were corporations.

"We haven't gotten hold of all of the documents yet, but Bland Sr. did finally confirm that his son had told him he would be getting an equity interest in return for being the front man and acting as owner on behalf of the group. That share agreement would take place once the deal was completed and the condos were built. He also confirmed that Robert might have been enticed into signing a note to compensate the group if he underperformed. Evidently it did fall on Robert to secure Builder's Risk Insurance, and he didn't do it adequately. Then there was a hurricane. Failing to insure the project adequately while under construction would certainly have been regarded as underperformance."

"So there could have been a motive to get rid of Robert if he both screwed up the insurance and then couldn't deliver on the equity to make at least part of it right."

"That's our guess. But we don't have any indications of who they might have sent, if they really did send someone, to take care of him. This would not have been a homegrown terrorist type of thing. It would have been some ten-thousand-dollar hit man from Miami who would have driven up, done the job and driven home. No trace. Plus, he would have just left the body, not put it in the car and taken it back to Miami. If the people who hired him wanted proof, he would just have taken a picture and brought them an ear or a finger or something."

"This is so un-Augusta County. Trophies around here are antlers, not fingers."

"You need to get out more. That's all I have for you now." Berry hung up.

This now tied Robert completely into the Turks deal and established a strong basis for a motive for that group to want to punish him and possibly Ashby and Caroline as well, if they had finally balked at fronting money to bail him out.

Herring called Kathryn and filled her in on what he had

learned. He would not see her until the weekend since she had
senior seminars and thesis reviews at school through Friday.
On Friday morning Berry called him to tell him that Ashby's
and Caroline's bodies would be released on Monday, and the
FBI would arrange for them to be delivered to a local funeral
home for burial or cremation. Herring reminded Berry that
Caroline's parents wanted no involvement with Ashby's funeral
or his family. He would tell Kathryn and get back to Berry on
where to have the body sent.

34

Inspection Sticker

Friday night Herring stayed at Kathryn's. They had agreed to go back to Monterey to tell Douglas about the release of the body in case he wanted to participate in any way. Herring went out with her on Saturday morning to help with the farm chores. He was given the task of using one of the tractors with a loader to move round hay bales to a pasture for some of the cows. The whole job was done from the comfort of a heated cab and with no more effort than it took to move levers that controlled the hydraulics of the tractor. It was about as far removed from his farm experience growing up as could be. He had to climb into a hay mow, throw down heavy square bales, tote them by hand to feed bunks, muscle his way between thousand-pound cows anxious to get at the hay, and then toss the bales into the bunk and cut away the twine while the cows tried to grab the first mouthfuls.

By ten they had finished chores and inspections, and by eleven thirty were through the gate and to the parking area next to Douglas's garage. Douglas was in the garage for a change, doing something under the truck when they pulled up.

He slid out. "I know it's not my charm and warmth. Why are you back here again so soon? Not that it isn't great to see you, Sis. And you, Sheriff."

Herring ignored the non-greeting. "What are you working on?"

"Tailpipe. I must have bumped a bracket on a rock on the road here. It just needed a splice and a new bracket."

"Where do you get something like that out here?"

"I don't. It's not the first time it's happened, so I keep a few repair parts on hand. A section of tailpipe, some bolts, a hacksaw, and a wrench. Actually, you can help. Start it up for me and let me see if the repair is leaking. It will put out a little exhaust smoke and condensation as it starts, and if it's leaking, I can see it."

Herring got into the cab and started the older Chevy. It started easily and ran smoothly. He noted that the truck had only 66,200 miles on the odometer. Douglas yelled for him to keep it running for a minute. While he was sitting there Herring noticed that the truck was due for an inspection in December. Out of curiosity he quietly opened the glove compartment and found the old inspection receipt and registration. The inspectors always recorded the mileage on the inspection date. The prior December, the odometer had shown 62,132 miles. If Douglas only used the truck to come to Kathryn's place or to Staunton monthly, that would have accounted for at most two thousand or so miles. That meant that in the past year Douglas had over two thousand unaccounted for miles on his pickup. And Herring had not seen any rocks on the road that could have damaged a tailpipe bracket. He quietly put the papers back in the glove compartment and closed it. At that point Douglas yelled that he could turn the engine off.

"All fixed."

"The engine sounds good. This was a very reliable engine for Chevy. Do you do the maintenance?"

"The simple stuff. No more than I use it, it's just an oil change and check fluids."

"Your inspection is almost due."

"I know. I'll get it done in time. You're quite observant. I guess it's your job."

"Seems to be."

Kathryn interjected. "I hate to interrupt this fascinating conversation, but we came to tell you father's body is going to be released on Monday. I've received a number of emails and a few actual cards and letters from people who knew him in the farm business and from the aircraft business. He planned to be buried at the old family plot at that little church north of town. The church is only used for special occasions, and you have to have had a plot there for ages to be able to be buried there. Given the circumstances, my plan is to do a quick private burial, no guests, probably Wednesday. Do you want to come over?"

Douglas was in the process of closing the garage and locking it. The door was exceptionally heavy, and he secured it with two sets of locks. "Some locals tried to break in a while back. I do use a tiny bit of technology from time to time. I saw who it was on a game camera. When they came back a second time something vandalized the wiring on their vehicle down by the gate. Bear? Raccoon? Hard to tell. Hard to replace and costly as well."

Game cameras. Interesting thought. There were all types. Douglas would not have been able to use a cellular type out here with no cell service, so he would have had to maintain some personal vigilance.

There was another layer to Douglas beyond that of isolated eccentric genius.

The all walked up to the house. Douglas and Kathryn had gone ahead and were chatting quietly. Herring had let them get ahead so as not to intrude on the conversations relative to the funeral.

When they got to the house, they went in to find the room quite toasty. Douglas had lit a fire in the cookstove, and a stew of some sort was simmering gently in the center of the cooking area. It was amazing to think that such a small firebox could heat an oven, a water reservoir, the cooking surface and even bread warmers over the main cook area. The kindling and starter wood supply was down, as was the little rick of dried oak. There were still some small pieces of pine kindling. And finally, the memory that had been trying to rise to the surface in Herring's brain slipped into place. The last time they had been here, the kindling rick had contained pieces of cut dried pine board. Such wood could have come from a construction site refuse pile. Herring sometimes got scraps of that type from sites to start his fireplace fires. But it was also the type of wood that the coffins had been made of, and at last count, only five of the six that had been ordered had been used.

35

Kindling

Douglas offered them some stew, and they took bowls outside to eat in the sun. Douglas and Kathryn continued to talk about the funeral and some items related to the estate. Kathryn had been too busy to meet with the attorneys relative to the will. She didn't know if there was anything in it for Douglas, but he didn't care and probably would not have taken any bequest. Herring was silent as he ate and did not respond to questions with much more than monosyllables.

It was arranged that Douglas would come over the night before the service and attend to support Kathryn. After lunch, they said goodbyes and headed down the path to the truck.

When they were out of range Kathryn turned to Herring. "What's up with you? You suddenly got very quiet back there."

"Let's talk in the car. I'm going to need to break all kinds of rules because I trust you. But we have to talk about what I fear."

"You are frightening me."

"I'm sorry. Let's get in the truck, and we can talk as we drive."

When they got through the gate and back to the highway, Herring began, "I have to ask again. You told me about his kinship with the deer in the woods, and his decision to become a vegetarian. But I have to ask again. Do you think Douglas is capable of killing someone?"

Kathryn looked at him, understanding the seriousness of the question. "Honestly, I don't know. I don't think he would ever harm anyone without serious cause. If he were confronted, I think he would defend himself. You can see that he's quite fit from all the work of just living out here on his own, and all of the biking and hiking and wood cutting and so on. Do you think he killed all of them?"

"No, I don't know what to think. I have to ask you something. I have never doubted what you said about where you were that weekend, but just swear to me one more time that you were really camping well away from the farm then."

Kathryn was silent. "If I were a different person, I could be completely incensed by you asking me that. But I think you have an idea, and you are really struggling with it, and I appreciate that integrity. It reminds me of Douglas's loyalty and it's a part of what attracted me to you. So I swear, I was camping, and I found the plane and the empty hangar that Saturday. And I *can* take you to the campsite and maybe even find the mushrooms again if they are still there." With that she reached over and squeezed his arm and left her hand there.

Herring was touched. His question could have cost him his relationship with her, and he had known that as he asked it, but he had to know. And he believed her answer.

"Alright, I'm going to tell you what was making me quiet, and how I think it adds up. First, we need to get some gas here in Monterey." They pulled into a Sunoco, a brand not widely seen at the intersection of 250 and 220. As Herring was filling the truck, his cell phone pinged back in service and a text from Berry appeared. Herring had never heard of a cell phone blowing up a gas station, but he'd seen the warnings on pumps, so he stepped away to read the text.

He finished filling the truck with fuel, got in the car and headed east on 250.

"Okay, I just had a text from Berry," said Herring. "And things got even weirder."

"How so?"

"Was Robert ever in your house at the farm?"

"It's possible. Early on maybe. I'd have to think. Back before Caroline threw the vase at me, we all pretended to get along for the sake of father. Not Douglas of course, but I was civil. We had a meal or two, and Robert and even the Bland's must have been there a couple of times. But some while ago. Why?"

"The techs apparently found a minute trace of Robert's blood on the floor in your bedroom. And also in the barn where you found the thumb drive."

"Holy shit! What was he doing in my bedroom? And how would they know it's Robert's blood? That is beyond creepy, Redd."

"To answer to your questions in reverse order, they matched Robert's DNA to Caroline's. So no doubt as to whose it is. As to being in your bedroom, if we assume—or really, we pretty much know—Robert was at the hangar around the time of the killings. There isn't any reason he couldn't have gone to either of the other houses afterward. Yours or the main house."

"Why?"

"Who knows why? I have a couple of ideas, though."

"Wait, back up. First, I want you to tell me why you got so quiet, and why you asked me whether Douglas could kill someone."

"Okay. But let me put it in the context of a scenario. Because I think Douglas has played a bigger role in this than anyone of us ever imagined."

"Oh Lord, no."

"I may be wrong, and honestly, unless he were to just up and tell us he did it, I don't think there is a shred of real evidence anywhere to tie him to any of it. But let me walk you through how I think it had to happen. You okay with that?"

"Sure, do I have a choice?"

"You can shoot holes in it as I go along."

"Alright, just tell me!" said Kathryn.

"First, I've wondered all along who staged the coffins and why. In the absence of any other evidence, I think they were done by Douglas."

"But why?"

"To scare your father into leaving the prenup as it was, and into leaving the trust alone."

"But the messages were asking for money. Besides, how could Douglas know?"

"You yourself told me that Douglas would come over and spend the night at your place a time or two every month or so, when Ashby and Caroline were going to be out of town, right?"

"Yes, but..."

"Was he with you a hundred percent of the time?"

"No, of course not, he's not into the cattle thing."

"So, he could easily have used your computer or the one up at the main house and found out anything he wanted. He has those skills. And he has the skills to do it and not leave a trace."

"But why would he bother?"

"Oh, I suspect he never ever trusted Caroline's motives in marrying your dad. He told us he despised her family, a visit or two ago, and you already knew it."

"Of course."

"I'm guessing he was always keeping an eye on things, to make sure your father and his new wife didn't screw you over. I think you are his only meaningful link to the real human world, and he would not tolerate any harm to you. Specifically not from people he despised."

"Put that way, I could come to agree with you. But what about the money requests?"

"I need to have the FBI people look at all of that more carefully, but my guess would be that those emails were not the only ones your father received. They may be contrived to hide the real messages."

"I don't follow."

"Your father would not have listened to Douglas if Douglas had straightforwardly asked him not to change the prenup. Right? I think we discussed this."

"That's most likely right. He probably wouldn't."

"Douglas had to blackmail him by threatening his reputation. That was the one thing Ashby would not have wanted to have happen. The coffin scenes meant everything to Ashby, but not to those who didn't know the history. The fact that Douglas had control of them would have been a powerful incentive for Ashby to cancel the prenup changes."

"That is some complicated psychological maneuvering you are postulating, Redd."

"For most people. Not Douglas. This is a guy who turns the pixels in one-hundred-fifty-year-old paintings into quilts, and has the patience to sew seven thousand pieces of cloth he dyed to just the right tint into a work of art. To arrange a couple of money orders and pick up and arrange a few coffins and some mannequins would be almost boringly simple for him. Besides, you asked why I was so quiet? When I was starting the truck for him, I looked at the inspection receipt from last December. That pickup has been driven several thousand miles that cannot be accounted for given what both of you have told me about his visits and habits."

"Well, I don't know everywhere he goes."

"That's probably true. But have you ever known him to put an extra two thousand miles on in a year? He keeps you up to date on most of what he does doesn't he?"

"Yes, I'm afraid I have to agree with you."

"There is one other thing that had been bothering me for the past week, and I couldn't put my finger on it. It was something I saw out of the corner of my eye that didn't fit, but I couldn't place it. Today I realized what it was."

"Something at the house."

"Yes, it was the kindling."

"You mean the kindling for the cook stove?"

"Yes, this time all of the kindling was pine branches that had been split by Douglas from trees in the area. He splits them again and again into tiny slivers almost. The last time, there were some pieces of commercial pine boards that had been chopped down into tiny starter pieces. It was the same kind of wood the coffins were made of, and we know one coffin isn't accounted for. I think he didn't want to waste the wood and cut it up to burn."

"Wow, that's a stretch. How could you ever prove that?"

"Oh, no way now. It's gone. And I imagine Douglas noticed me looking and probably realized the mistake. But if there was any of the coffin left, he probably burned it this afternoon."

"So you think the kindling and the miles prove my brother staged the coffins. Do you think he killed the three of them? I can't fathom that."

"I don't think he killed your father and Caroline. I think that either Robert, or Robert and a partner, killed the two of them. I think there is still the remote possibility, but not high, that Robert was accompanied initially by someone from the Turks group. My guess is that something went wrong when Ashby landed. A quarrel, a struggle, maybe Ashby was armed, I don't know. The person who could most likely tell us, Robert, is missing, and I am guessing dead."

Kathryn thought about that for a bit. "I can see that, the way you describe it. I can see it more easily if Robert had someone with him who was more cold-blooded. But I didn't know Robert well enough to say if he could do it or not."

"If he was in danger because of his screwup in Turks, that could have made him desperate enough I suppose," said Herring. "At any rate, he was there, according to his phone. I think we can establish that much. For now, let's just agree on that for arguments sake."

"Agreed. Now what happened next in your scenario?"

"Is there any way to know if Douglas might have been at the farm that weekend without you knowing?"

"We could always ask him. But if he was, and if he was involved, I don't know why he would admit it."

"I suppose that's right. But he didn't say anything to you about coming over? Did he know you were going camping?"

"Yes, I'm pretty sure he did. I had been out to his place the week before to take him some groceries and hang out. I told him I was doing a wilderness hike and that I was going to camp alone for a couple of nights."

"I think we should at least ask him. But there are only two scenarios that make much sense if everything else we have postulated is true. One, an associate of Robert's killed him after he failed with Ashby. I honestly doubt that for two reasons. First there is no evidence of another person being there. Second, it doesn't explain Robert's blood in your bedroom. Why wouldn't the partner just shoot Robert and leave him in the hangar?"

"You think Douglas encountered Robert at my house, and killed him?"

"I would put a lot of money on it. Nothing else holds together."

"So where is his body? And why make it disappear?"

Part Five

36

Conjecturing

"I am probably overthinking this, but I believe that Douglas surprised Robert in your house, maybe cleaning himself up or possibly planting a gun to incriminate you. Robert was certainly in your house and is now gone. Who knows?"

"You are in the land of make believe now, Redd."

"Maybe, maybe not. Let's accept that Douglas surprised him and killed him. Maybe even self-defense. In fact, most likely self-defense if Robert had just killed Ashby and his own sister."

"But why not just call the police then?"

"Because, Douglas had just been given the perfect set of circumstances. If he worked quickly, he could wrap up a story he had begun, and leave us all in the dark. Evil punished, and you financially stable."

"I don't follow."

"Sure you do, if you think about. Douglas might well have heard the shots and figured out what happened at the hangar. Either way after his run-in with Robert he goes to the hangar, finds the two bodies. He can now tie the warnings to the killings by putting the two bodies in two of the coffins. He cleans them in the processing shed, wraps them with cotton in the style of a Muslim burial, and puts them in the body bags and coffins and stages them. Now it looks like a terrorist group did it."

"Why not leave Robert there as well?"

"That wouldn't fit. Robert was never a part of the Iraqi event, may never have even known about it. The Iraqi scenes in the coffins were meant to stop your father from giving Robert money that should have been, and is, yours. That is the final link. I am guessing Douglas loaded Robert's body into his pickup in a sheet of white hay plastic and buried him somewhere up on that mountain that we will never find. Or on someone else's mountain."

"You are making my head swim once again. I really need to think about this. Are you going to tell Berry your theory?"

"I don't know. In some ways I think I have to because not telling leaves me and you hanging morally. I can't prove anything, not a single bit of what I just told you. Douglas would have to come forward and confess, and he is never going to do that. But we almost have to let Berry have a go at it."

"What if he finds and proves that Douglas did it?"

"That was always a chance that Douglas was taking, from the very beginning. And he was willing to take it. Not necessarily that someone would get killed, but that something unpleasant could and probably would come out of this. I will tell Berry that I think Robert killed Ashby and Caroline, and then either disappeared or his colleagues from Turks got him. I imagine that is what Berry thinks anyway. He is so deep into conspiracy on a daily basis he will make something of the coffin warnings that fits his model. But I also think Douglas is clever enough that he has covered his tracks. If he actually did all of this, he will not be found out."

"That may be the case, but you think you figured it out. Why wouldn't Berry or the FBI?"

"First of all, I am just conjecturing, and most of what I am proposing is based on a few extra miles on a truck odometer and a piece of wood that no longer exists. If not for those two things, I would not be at this point. Well, there was a barely recognizable wince at the word 'arrest' a few days back, but that's all. I think it is a dead end, or circumstantial at best."

"Why would you do it this way? Because of me? I don't want you to do this and then begin to resent me. Or have every visit with Douglas be strained or impossible."

"Kathryn, bits of this scenario and several others have been bouncing around in my head for the past week. I am totally at peace with this. If this is how it happened, I am actually impressed with Douglas's ability to pull it off. And I admire loyalty. And I especially admire loyalty when the person exhibiting it has had to overcome obstacles that most of us never have to address. Douglas's life has probably not been easy with his spectrum. Am I right?"

"More than you know."

"So, I see nothing to be gained from subjecting him to an arrest and investigation that would go nowhere. I don't think I even have enough to get a warrant if I wanted to pursue this. I really have nothing to go on."

The Killer

Douglas had been up at the main house going through his dad's files when he heard the plane land. Caroline and Winston stepped down and walked in past a MINI Cooper that had pulled up next to the hangar. Fearing he might be caught in the act he had quickly shut down the computer. He thought he heard some shots, but they were muffled, and the sound of gunfire was common in the autumn during hunting season. He stepped to the front of the house and saw someone come out of the hangar and get into the car. The car turned and drove back to the road and turned left, drove a short distance, and turned right toward Kathryn's house. Douglas quickly jumped into his pickup and headed in the same direction. When he got to Kathryn's house, the car he had seen at the hangar was in the driveway. He cut the engine to his pickup, drifted in behind the car, got out and went in.

Robert turned at the sound of footsteps to find Douglas standing in the doorway of Kathryn's bedroom.

"What the fuck are you doing here, Douglas?"

"I don't think that's the right question. What the fuck are you doing here, in my sister's house?" At that point he noticed the gun in Robert's hand and the open quilt chest at the foot of the bed. He understood, instantly. "What have you done? You were about to put that gun in that chest."

Robert dropped the cover to the chest and lunged at Douglas, tripping on the edge of a throw rug and landing on his side just in front of Douglas. Douglas was enraged. This idiot had been trying to set up his sister for a crime she did not commit.

As Robert landed on the wood floor, Douglas fell on him with his knees to Robert's chest, forcing the air out of him. Robert still held the gun, and in spite of having his breath taken away, he managed to lift it up. Douglas, with all of his outdoor work, hiking, and biking, was much stronger than Robert. He seized Robert's arm and slowly turned it until the gun pointed at Robert's head.

"No, no, stop," Robert breathlessly squeaked out. But Douglas was determined to end this. Robert had just tried to frame his sister and attempted to kill him. He had known from the emails the trouble Robert was in, and knew what his father was trying to do to get the money to bail him out. He had not expected Robert to show up. Seeing Robert with the gun, he assumed Ashby and Caroline were now dead.

He continued to force the gun back on Robert, whose finger was caught in the trigger guard. The gun was now pointed almost directly at Robert's left eye. One more push and the gun fired, directly through the eye and into Robert's brain. Robert let out a sigh and was gone. A trickle of blood and aqueous liquid ran down the side of Robert's face. The other eye was open and staring.

Douglas released the arm and the hand holding the gun. He stood up and looked at what he had done. He felt strangely distant from it. But at the same time, the mind that could design computer chips and operating systems, and turn a hundred-fifty-year-old painting into a seven-thousand-piece quilt, handily pieced together what needed to be done and the steps needed to do it.

He went into Kathryn's bathroom, grabbed a towel, and wrapped it around Robert's head to prevent any more blood from getting onto the floor. He then dragged the body down the hall and out onto the patio. He moved his truck and found that Robert had left the keys in the car he drove, so started it and turned it around. Keeping an eye out for passing cars, he managed to lift Robert's body onto his shoulder, carry it out to the drive, and put it in the trunk of the car. He needed to find out what had happened to his father and Caroline. He chose to take the car and leave his truck at Kathryn's house. He drove back to the hangar, got out, and slid the left door open. Inside he found the two bodies. He quickly opened the door wider and drove the car into the hangar and pulled the doors shut and locked them behind him.

It was now just after four in the afternoon. Douglas had been on the farm enough weekends with Kathryn to know the sched-ule. He knew that barring an emergency, there would be no one around the farm until the next morning. She had told him she was going camping when they were together the week before. His first thought was to check for electronics. He found Robert's phone in a pants pocket and took out the battery and pried out the SIM card, disabling it completely. Douglas went out to the plane *and retrieved his dad's laptop, his cell phone, and Caroline's. He disabled them both.*

He had planned to place another coffin in town that night. It would hold only the photos of Ashby's murderous acts. He would send Ashby a final email warning that he would receive when he landed in Europe the next morning. If Ashby persisted with changing his prenup and estate documents when he got back from Europe, Douglas would stage the last two coffins with mannequins resembling his father and Caroline, and publicize his father's incriminating deeds. He had that night's coffin kit and his bicycle in the bed of his pickup under a tarp. It now registered with him that he could play out the scenario using the real bodies. It would not have the same humiliation effect since Ashby was already dead, but it would perpetuate the terrorist angle and keep himself and Kathryn off the suspect list. He would need to prep the bodies, go back to Monterey for a second coffin kit, and decide where to leave the coffins and what to do with Robert's car and Robert. He was amply aware of DNA tracing and with not using his truck to move bodies. Fortunately, he had the rental car.

He had the rest of the evening and the night to do what he needed to do. That is if everything went as usual and there were no unexpected visitors to the farm, and Kathryn didn't change her mind and come back early.

Douglas first took one of the utility carts that was in the hangar and loaded Ashby's body onto it. He opened a small door and wheeled the body down to the veterinary hospital and left the body on the floor. He next brought Caroline's body down and left her by Ashby.

He used an overhead lifting device, usually used for lifting calves, to put the bodies on a stainless-steel table in the main examining room of the veterinary unit. He stripped both bodies, bagged the soiled clothes, and washed the bodies down. He left them on the table to dry and took the bagged clothes with him to burn.

Douglas locked the veterinary shed. It was now getting dark. He went back to the hangar and opened Ashby's computer. There was a decent signal even here due to the router that was based in the hangar for the farm records. He found the United site where Ashby had made the reservations for Europe and cancelled the entire itinerary. This would add an element of confusion. It also occurred to him that Ashby not making the flight might raise some questions somewhere, and someone might come to the farm. The presence of the rental car might help with confusion, but not if Robert's body was found in the trunk. He drove the car to one of the outer barns further down the road, took the body out of the car, and rolled it in plastic wrap that he cut from a hay bale. He left the body behind some stacked hay bales with more loose hay tossed over it. He drove the car back to the farm.

He then walked back to Kathryn's house, got in his pickup, and drove back to his garage. He picked up one of the last two coffin kits, two body bags, and the last two mannequins that were hidden in the woods beyond the garage under tarps and brush. He had not decided yet what to do with Robert's body or the mannequins. He already had the roll of cotton material and his bicycle in the pickup bed.

He drove back to Centennial Farm, used the hoist to help put the two bodies into the body bags, poured in a bit of cattle disinfectant to kill odors, and used the cart to haul the bodies one at a time to the arena. In the hangar, he assembled two of the coffins and carried them over to the arena. He placed the bodies in them, screwed them shut, and used a rake to rake the sawdust around them. He found some cleaning supplies in the office and wiped the floor to remove any footprints. The rest of the surfaces were dusty, and the clean floor would stand out, but he couldn't help that.

On his drive back to Centennial, he had concluded that both the car and Robert's body would have to be hidden or disposed of. He could not risk burying Robert on his land or in having the car found and checked for DNA. Burning would be best, but that would attract attention and he was viscerally opposed to the pollution it would cause. He was also uncomfortable with the desecration of Robert's corpse, but he didn't have time or a place to bury the body, and the car had to disappear.

He finally decided that he would place the body back in the trunk of the car, along with the bag of clothes he'd removed from Caroline and his father, and drive it all to the old mines above the town of Crimora. By laying the front passenger seat down, he was able to awkwardly load his bike straddling the front and back. There were several open pits that remained after the manganese mine was closed in the mid-fifties, and which were now full of water. Some pits had been landscaped and the surrounding land turned into home sites, but at least one, which was several hundred feet deep, was secluded but could be accessed from an old mine access road. He would have to send the car to the bottom with the body in the trunk and bike back to the farm. It would take only an hour or so.

By the time Douglas finished with placing the two coffins in the arena and preparing to retrieve Robert's body from the outer barn, it was nearly ten at night. He placed the body in a remaining bag and put it in the trunk of the rental, relocked the barn, drove to the mines, disposed of the car, and biked back to Centennial. It was now close to midnight, but he believed he had done all he could to establish a scene that would support either murders by domestic terrorists or by supporters of the Turks group.

The two mannequins were still in his truck bed. He drove to Staunton and got on I-64 and drove east to the first shopping center he came to in Richmond, Willow Lawn. He pulled around behind the mall and tossed the two mannequins into a dumpster. He got a cup of coffee at an all-night fast-food drive through and headed home. Over the next couple days, he would burn the sixth coffin kit in his woodstove.

Epilogue

The following morning, Herring called Berry and gave him his take on Robert having killed the Ashby's and suggesting that Douglas could have been involved, but that it was only conjecture on his part and that he had no evidence. Berry's team did follow up, but as Herring had predicted, they found nothing that could link Douglas to the scene at the time. His DNA was found around the farm but always at places he would have been with Kathryn at some point. Nothing was found at his house in the mountains.

Acknowledgments

I would like to thank two individuals for their guidance and support in the writing of this book. First, many thanks to Kim Sherman, who diligently read the chapters as I produced them and encouraged me to complete the book before going back and messing with it. And second, thanks to Kitty Sachs, whose detailed and thorough editing turned this manuscript into a readable volume.